Samantha Bentley's parents eloped to Norfolk from the Midlands. She was born and raised in Norfolk within a large family of five sisters. Samantha has always painted and created, but didn't attempt writing seriously until the lockdown presented her with the time to put pen to paper. She moved away from Norfolk for a few years, but the pull of her home county and the sea drew her back.

Samantha Bentley

THE BEACH CAFÉ

AUSTIN MACAULEY PUBLISHERS™

LONDON • CAMBRIDGE • NEW YORK • SHARJAH

A CIP catalogue record for this title is available from the British Library.

ISBN 9781398484870 (Paperback)
ISBN 9781398484887 (ePub e-book)

www.austinmacauley.com

First Published 2023
Austin Macauley Publishers Ltd®
1 Canada Square
Canary Wharf
London
E14 5AA

A big thank you to Austin Macauley Publishers and all the staff; you have been with me and supported me every step of the way.

To my dearest friend, Lisa Baldock, thank you for so much!

Also, thank you to my three beautiful daughters for all your support and my dear mum, who inspired Maggie.

A big thank also to one of my oldest friends, Steve Lockwood, for his support.

Anna was heading towards her 50th birthday; she was separating from her husband after 20 years together, her marriage had grown loveless. She was unfulfilled in her dead-end job and her children had grown and flown the nest, now was time for a change.

Anna had climbed up the management ladder and then climbed back down. She had spent most of the last 20 years concentrating on being a wife and a mother, and for too long she had put her needs after that of others. That chapter of her life needed to and was about to end.

One thing she knew for certain, she didn't need or want a man, she had spent more than 30 of her 50 years in long-term and controlling relationships. She wanted some time alone, she wanted to find herself again, the person she was, the confident and spirited individual she had been and she wanted to do it on her terms, at her speed, and however which way she chose.

Chapter 1
Moving On

The First Day of the Rest of Your Life

The marriage split, house sale and all the wrangles that had gone on over the last few months had taken their toll on her. Anna had moved all her belongings into storage apart from a few large bags and the odd items packed into her car. She had given notice to her dread end job, and decided to use the small amount of money from the house sale to take some time out and decide what her next steps would be.

She had rented a small cottage on the Norfolk coast and she was looking forward to stacking the dishwasher incorrectly, getting into her jim-jams at 2pm and locking the front door with the knowledge that no-one would be letting themselves in, bringing their doom, gloom, threats and constant criticism with them.

This was going to be her time, she would live in her naturally positive frame of mind; there would be no irritating and habitual clearing of the throat, that irritating grunt was banished from her new home. She wanted some peace and tranquility and the only company she needed was that of her dog, Teddy.

As Anna pulled away from the house for the last time with her trusted cockapoo in tow, she took one last glance at the house she had spent so many Christmases in, where her last child was born and where she had laughed, cried and made so many good memories. The dawning of her future suddenly scared her and she felt a sadness, could she have made it work?

Anna quickly shook herself out of those sort of thoughts. There were 2 people in their marriage and he had stopped trying many years ago. With that, she put the car into gear and drove away. Anna felt her heart swell heavy as a warm tear ran down her flushed cheek. She was filled with a strange feeling of sadness, fear, relief and joy as she turned out of the close for the very last time.

She felt a sadness for her once loving marriage and for the family life which would change for her children, but overall she felt a little know feeling of freedom as she pressed down on the accelerator and drove away from the saddening cage which was her married life.

The sun was shining on a late summer morning as she drove towards the Norfolk coast; she had spent most of her life in Norfolk. Anna had been born and grew there and although she had moved around a lot in her youth, she had moved back to the familiar and laid back life of Norfolk in her late 20s, and settled in the suburbs of Norwich where she met, married and grew her family.

The journey would take about 40 minutes, but Anna was in no hurry, she was finally the owner of her own destiny and although she felt pangs of fear creep in, she breathed deeply and let the sweet smell of the hedgerows waft through the car window as she took the picturesque back route to her new home, telling herself that all would be well.

She had to believe in herself and find the confident and self-assured person she was in her 20s and 30s, the one who had slowly ebbed away. She knew she was in there somewhere and she was determined to find her.

Anna pulled into the car park at the familiar seaside town of Cromer where she had often visited with her parents on holidays. Memories flooded back of happy times in the safety of her childhood family. She had lost both her parents in the last few years and the familiar feelings were welcome on this day.

Anna had always wanted to live by the sea and a few months back while walking Teddy along the coast, she had happened upon a small wooden clad cottage overlooking the sea, in a small village not far from the town. Anna had called the number on the for-let sign, viewed and agreed on renting the small beach house. Today was move-in day, she put Teddy on his lead and headed towards the Estate Agents to collect the keys.

On entering, a friendly young lady recognized her and headed to get her the keys. Anna stood and waited as Teddy sniffed around; she hoped he would not disgrace her, like he had in the garden center by poohing on the artificial grass in the posh internal garden furniture display. Anna held her hand out for the keys as the young lady walked towards her.

She felt a pang of fear again; she waived it away and took the keys, thanking the young lady and heading out of the agent's office with the new home keys in her pocket. She rubbed the large worn wooden keyring and wondered how soon this would feel familiar and could she actually do this? Could she live alone, after being so use to having a busy family home, had she been fooling herself?

Before any panic set in, Anna steered herself to follow the plan and headed towards Davies Fish shop on the bustling garden street that lead to the sea. Her father had always stopped to collect a crab from the same shop, whenever they visited or travelled near to Cromer.

Being a nice summer day, the town was filled with families of holiday makers and day trippers. There was a smell of hot candyfloss and fish and chips in the air. The children jumped around in excitement carrying their newly purchased buckets and spades in numerous bright colors as the parents juggled bags, windbreaks and all the essential supplies for a day on the beach. There was the sound of laughter, happy chat, gulls and the faint tinkling of flags on metal masts—a traditional English seaside sound, if there was such a thing.

Shellfish had always been a favorite of Anna's beloved father who had been a kind, strong and honorable man. She missed him dearly; he liked the simpler things in life, like walks on the beach. He loved his family but he was also happy in his own company and Anna was thankful that she, like her father, enjoyed being alone. She just hoped she would be ok with how alone she was going to be.

Every Saturday, her father would take her to the local market to spend her pocket money and pick up a fresh Cromer crab, cockles, mussels and prawns. He would spend the afternoon at the kitchen table, picking and preparing the shellfish. Anna had fond memories of helping her father as a small child, she was given the tiny crab legs, to pick out the sweet white meat with her tiny fingers; he would smile when he noticed her eating some of the sweet meat she had picked out.

Life seemed so slow and simple back then. Anna didn't really feel any different today however, so many years had passed and at such a speed, she still felt like that small child going to collect the crab but now her parents were gone and she was a single grown woman.

The fish shop with its Blue and white striped awning had hardly changed since her childhood, with paintings and yellowed photos of fishing boats, old fishing nets and crab baskets hung from the ceiling and walls and the large glass fronted chillers proudly displaying todays catch of brown crabs, lobster, cockles, samphire, prawns and numerous other fish and shell fish.

There would always be onlookers peering through the old shop window, unsure of what you would do with such crustaceans. If you didn't have time or know how to pick out your own crab meat, you would ask for a dressed crab. As Anna had all the time in the world, she asked for a large fine looking plump brown crab, undressed and as always, she was asked if she would like ice which came in small white plastic bags, sealed as you would a loaf of bread.

How many bags would depend on your journey, when asked, Anna replied, "No, thank you. I'm local," which raised the eyebrow of the imposing and tall lady in her thick white plastic clad apron, who clearly did not recognize her. *Yet,* thought Anna. There was still an old chest freezer to the side of the shop entrance with piles of newspapers on; here you could wrap your purchase with or without ice to keep it fresh for the journey home.

Pleased with her purchase, as crab availability was dependent on the days catch, weather, season etc., Anna headed next door to the bakers for some fresh bread, then for a wonder around what would now be her new home town.

Her plan was to collect the keys, pick up a Cromer Crab and once settled into the cottage, go for a walk along the beach to the front of the cottage, then spend the rest of the afternoon pottering and leisurely picking the crab with a cool glass of G&T in her jimmies. 'Bliss', she thought with a hint of trepidation.

The cottage she was renting used to be a holiday let, but the elderly owners who lived close by had become tired of managing it and put it up for a long term rental to the right person. Thankfully, they had deemed her the right candidate for the cottage. It was simply furnished and reached via a small road at the back of the cottage through the costal dunes, with a sprinkling of other houses and a view across the beach and down to the sea.

Pulling up to her new home filled Anna with excitement, stepping out of the car and letting Teddy jump out and eagerly sniff around to investigate, Anna unloaded the contents of the car and the essentials she had bought with her, including her favorite Gin and the glasses she has purchased on holiday in Malta with a girlfriend last year, where realization that her marriage was over had hit her; i.e. he had decided to go hiking with his mates rather than holiday with her.

Anna fondly remembered the evenings sipping their favorite tipple on the hotel balcony, talking long into the night; it was the best holiday she had had in a very long time. Another realization of how loveless her marriage had become. She had carefully transported the two glasses home.

Her soon to be ex-husband had also favored the glasses, using one for his evening tipple. Anna had brought both glasses with her in some sort of independent defiance.

The cottage was pleasant and light, a little dilapidated but nothing a bit of TLC couldn't fix. Downstairs was open plan, the kitchen had a basic but workable layout, complete with a small dishwasher which would always be stacked incorrectly! In the center of the room was a small table and chairs, there was a sofa, a coffee table and an armchair, a wood burning stove and French windows which looked out to sea and opened onto a small deck.

Anna unpacked and headed out to walk along the beach with Teddy, basking in the afternoon sun and enjoying the breeze coming off the waives. There were a few walkers on the beach but not too many. Anna decided not to walk too far as it had been a long day, so she headed back to the cottage, happy with the freedom she felt and the sight, sound and smell that the sea gave her.

As she walked around the seashore, she caught sight of her little cottage and her heart jumped a beat. This was her new home, she had made it, she felt free.

Back at the cottage, Anna showered and changed into a comfortable and cool jersey night slip and a thin dressing gown, it was too warm for jimmies. She poured herself a large G&T and stood in the open French doors, leant against the frame and looked out to sea as Teddy settled in his bed, tired after the day's exertions.

Anna could see the walkers on the beach and the children playing chase with the waves. She could faintly hear their joyous laughter as they got their feet wet or had a close shave and the deeper laughter of the parents in response to their antics. They were close enough to make her feel somehow safe and connected but far enough away to give her seclusion, so far she felt this was a good first step forward.

Anna laid the newspaper wrapping of the crab on the table and positioned her chair so she could look out to sea when she looked up from picking the crab. She had the usual array of utensils for cracking and picking and set about the methodical task with the sound of the walkers and the sea lapping coming through the open doors.

She took her time as Teddy stirred, making contented noises as he dreamt of his beach run. That evening, Anna sat in silence eating the crab with the fresh bread and butter and a glass of the chilled white wine, the owners had left in her fridge as a homecoming gift. Later, Anna fell asleep with her bedroom window open.

Teddy snuggled beside her as he always did, both lulled to sleep by the sound of the ocean and tired from the activities of the day.

Chapter 2
A New Day Is Dawning

Anna was woken early by the sun shining through the thin bedroom curtains. As she became alert to her new surroundings, she smiled to herself; today she could decide whatever she wished to do and change her mind if she wanted to, as many times as she wished. The sound of the waves and walkers on the beach gladdened her. She didn't think she would ever tire of that sound.

Starting her new morning routine was a joy to Anna. She let Teddy out and switched on the kettle. Anna settled on the comfy chair in front of the picture window to watch the beach's morning ritual unfold. She wondered how many regulars she would start to notice.

There was a lady with a whippet, looking relaxed but with purpose, an older couple walking slowly arm in arm, looking very much in love, maybe they had cracked it, been married for years but still in love. Anna felt a tinge of sadness thinking of the love her husband had once had for her; where had it gone wrong?

She quickly dismissed the thought and went to get dressed, ready to create her own beach routine with Teddy, a morning walk along the beach.

Stepping out, Anna breathed in the fresh sea air as Teddy ran ahead to investigate. They walked without thinking for what must have been half an hour, taking in the new soundings they would call home. Anna stopped to chat to an older lady walking a very slow and slightly overweight basset hound named Barbara.

She lived on the beach also and had done for many years. She offered to give Anna the low down on the comings and goings of the area over a cup of tea at her house. They exchanged details and agreed on tomorrow afternoon at 2pm. Her name was Maggie; she was very chatty and bubbly and seemed to know everything about everyone. Anna felt she would enjoy Maggie's company.

As they parted, she heard Maggie greeting another walker with great enthusiasm. She glanced down at Barbara who looked less enthusiastic and slumped down on the sand with a long deep sigh which made Anna smile.

Anna headed back to the cottage to plan for the day. Stepping into the cottage gave her such solace, she had all the joy the ocean could give, with the peace and tranquility of her own little haven. She settled down on the sofa with another cup of tea to put together a list of all that she needed.

She would head into town shortly to get the items and have a mooch around. Teddy was already asleep on his bed in front of the French windows, tired from his mornings investigations.

Anna parked up and headed for the hardware store on Church Street, which she remembered as being an Aladdin's cave. She was not wrong, they sold everything and anything, from drills to picnic baskets, chef knives, rope, bread bins, woks, decorative plates; you name it, they had it. Anna picked up some white paint, brushes and few other bits and bobs.

Having dropped the items at the car, she headed to Garden street to have a look in the shops to see if she could find some items to brighten up her little cottage. She picked up a driftwood lamp and nice rug. After visiting the supermarket for the other items on her list, she headed home.

Teddy was happy to see her as always, bringing one of her slippers, then running away with it again. After unpacking and setting out her new items, Anna breathed in her little cottage loving every inch of it. She found the view of the ocean mesmerizing. The weather had turned slightly and she could see dark clouds coming in from the horizon.

Watching a whole weather front move in made her feel very much at one with the world, safe in her little beach house looking out to the ocean. She lit the wood burner for the first time and sat on her new rug in front of it with a G&T, watching the ocean roll in and out. Teddy laid beside her with his head laid in her lap.

Anna enjoyed the freedom of her new routine. At some point, she may make some dinner or maybe just toast, she was yet to decide. Anna had expected to feel lonely, but she found herself far from it; she felt contented and home. She had made the right decision and she loved living it.

Anna rose early again the next morning to give her cottage a lick of clean white paint, before showering and heading out to visit Maggie. Anna still delighted in stepping out of her front door and onto the beach, the sun was shining and there was a refreshing light breeze. Maggie's was a short 20 minute meander up the beach.

Maggie's beach house was a large and grand affair, sitting on stilts much higher than the average, with a large raised deck with a glass and rope balustrade. There were large and comfortable, cushioned garden sofas sat either side of a chunky glass topped coffee table. The house was painted grey and white and large classic but ornate lights framed either side of the large glass bi-folding doors.

The upstairs boasted a large full height triangular picture window which made the most of the views. Anna could also see 2 comfy looking, oversized armchairs, also positioned to enjoy the view, a large ornate light fitting was hanging in the eves made up of many glass domes of all shapes and sizes hanging at different levels. This spoke 'I am a grand beach hut, made to be admired'.

Maggie waved and beckoned from the deck, Barbara was lounging on the sofa beside Maggie. She motioned Anna to sit on the sofa opposite and thanked her for bottle of wine Anna gave to her. "Wonderful," pronounced Maggie. "I can see we are going to get on!"

Maggie already had a pot of tea, cups and saucers set up on a mirrored tray on the coffee table. She busied herself putting the wine in the fringe and poured the tea. "Now, tell me all about you," she declared, flamboyantly getting comfortable by laying back into her sofa as though this was going to take some time!

As Anna started to tell her story, coyly at first, the flood gates opened. She had a feeling Maggie knew this may happen as she passed her the box of tissues already placed artfully on the coffee table beside the ornate bunch of fresh flowers which wafted its sweet scent in the breeze. It did indeed take a long time, there was a pause as Maggie fetched the wine and asked many questions.

As Maggie artfully drew out Anna's inner feelings, by the end of it Maggie knew Anna inside and out. As Anna's story came to a close, Maggie looked on her with kindness. "You have come to the right place to rejuvenate and re-invent yourself, my dear. More wine?" Maggie asked.

They talked into the evening. Maggie miraculously producing a platter of food to nibble on while she gave her the low down on anyone who walked by. Maggie had moved here from London after her husband died 10 years ago and she played quite a big part in the local community, so there was not much she didn't know.

Anna was interested in getting to know her neighbors and what was available and dog friendly in the local area. Maggie agreed to meet Anna the next morning for a walk along the beach. They would meet at Anna's and head in the opposite direction. Anna realized Maggie was going to be a close and trusted friend.

The next morning, Anna stood on her small deck savoring the last of her morning cup of tea and watching the waves ebb in and out as she caught sight of Maggie coming up the beach with a big smile on her face. "Morning, dear Anna," she called when close enough to be heard. Barbara was nowhere to be seen.

Maggie explained that sensing a long walk, Barbara had refused to cross the threshold, padded over to her bed and slumped down with her back to Maggie. "Barbara does as Barbara wishes," Maggie stated with a wry smile on her face.

The two of them with Teddy in tow, headed along the beach. Anna's immediate neighbors were the owners of her own cottage. Waves were exchanged, Anna saw Maggie, acknowledge with a nod towards the couple and received a smile and nod back. It was a knowing exchange, like Anna was being officially introduced into society as an accepted member of the community, as decreed by Maggie.

This made Anna smile. She liked Maggie and knew she was in safe hands. Maggie gave the low down on the next few beach houses—a family from London who rarely came, an older gentleman called Harry, who lost his wife a couple of years ago also waved as they walked by. The next hut was run down and sad looking. Maggie explained it used to be a thriving beach café run by Harry's wife and daughter.

Maggie explained that the daughter did not want to take it on after Harry's wife died and Harry did not have the heart to part with it. As Harry couldn't maintain it, it was slowly allowing the sea air to take its toll. "That's so sad," Anna said.

"Yes, indeed. What are your plans, Anna?" *Subtle*, thought Anna with a smile, but Anna was intrigued by the little café. The two of them stood looking at the run down building for quite a few moments.

"I've not thought that far ahead, it's one day at a time right now. I took the cottage to clear my head but there will come a time when I will need to find an income of some sort," a question her daughters posed on every phone call. Anna could hear the cogs in Maggie's head wearing and she didn't mind a bit, her mind's cogs were also wearing. Anna liked the look of the little café, alone and neglected.

"The café was a little haven for beach walkers, especially when the weather was bad. It's been sorely missed since it closed," said Maggie.

They walked on past the next few cottages and a cut which led to a beach car park which was roughly dug out of the dunes before they decided to head back. It was mid-morning and dark clouds were threatening; they walked back chatting away. Anna felt happy in Maggie's presence and she already felt a part of the community.

Waves were exchanged with the beach side residents as they headed back and Anna wondered whether this stop gap might prove to be more of a stopping point. As they reached Anna's cottage, the two said their goodbyes and agreed on another walk in a couple of days' time. Maggie marched off towards her glam shack, as Anna had called it, in her head of course.

Anna spent a happy afternoon pottering in the cottage, watching the walkers on the beach and the weather fronts come and go. As the evening fell she lit the log burner and sat snuggled with Teddy as the sun set on the ocean.

Chapter 3
Settling In

Anna had spent the last few days making her cottage as homely as possible. She had freshened it up with a new coat of white paint, put up new curtains and blinds and added some finishing touches. She had also been to her storage lock-up and brought back some of her own furniture and furnishings, which she couldn't fit into her car on move day.

Anna had given the deck a makeover. It was larger than she thought after she had cleared all the old, rickety furniture and rubbish that had built up over time. She had sanded, painted and replaced the threads that were once the rope balustrade. New furniture had been added and it was now a wonderful place to sit, relax and eat. Even her neighbors had commentated on how much better it looked.

She had walked with Maggie a couple of times and had lunch with her in Cromer. She had met more of the locals and now knew most of the residents living in the properties close to her by name. Teddy was also making friends. He would run up to the owners' cottages and say hello.

She had been invited for tea at a few, but Teddy's favorite was Harry, who owned the run down café. Teddy would bound up the stairs of Harry's deck to see if he was in. Harry himself had taken to carrying dog treats in his pocked, probably part of the reason Teddy liked him so much.

Today was Sunday and her daughters were coming to visit. Anna had two daughters—Molly, who was at university studying art; she lived with several other students in a house share. Molly was very laid back and a bit bohemian. As a child, she did not care what she looked like and not much had changed today.

Anna remembered one morning before school looking at Molly and her wild wavy long locks and asking, "Have you brushed your hair this morning?"

To which Molly replied, "Yes…with my fingers," she had stated as she skipped out the door. She was kind, sweet and had an amazing imagination. Nothing phased Molly, she took everything in her stride.

Emily, or Em for short, was more cautious. She did not like change or new situations. She worked in the city with her fiancé and everything she did was considered, re-thought and re-thought again. Em was not keen on Anna moving to the coast, she saw it as outlandish. She felt Anna should buy another house in suburbia and stay as she had been.

Anna was busy cooking up sausage rolls, snacks and cakes so the visit could be leisurely. The plan was to take a walk on the beach and then sit on the deck and have a picnic and watch the world go by. Anna was renowned for her sausage rolls, as was her mother who used to bake them for the local WI market.

Anna had made enough so both girls could take some home. Molly was travelling up with Em, as this was their first visit the girls were coming alone. The cottage did have 2 bedrooms and a small bathroom but today was just a day visit to see where their mum had decided to call home.

Em's car pulled up outside the cottage late morning. Teddy had heard the car and was eagerly wagging his tail at the door. Anna opened the door and Teddy shot out to greet the girls, he had become a part of the family when the girls still lived at home.

The girls made a fuss of Teddy and he jumped up with glee between each sister then back again. Molly bounded into the cottage first, pronounced 'Cool', ran and launched herself across the room onto the comfy chair by the French window. Teddy jumped up and snuggled in beside her with a sigh.

Em still stood at the car purveying the cottage. Anna could see she was not so amused, but Em smiled and headed in, slowly wondering around the cottage and taking in all the details. Em was asking lots of questions like, "What about when it gets cold," and "don't you feel scared here all on your own." Every so often raucous laughter would come from Molly as she watched the beach antics.

"There's a dog trying to do rude stuff to another dog," "An old lady tried to run from the wave and got it soooo wrong!" Molly was delighting in the comings and goings on the beach, which lightened the mood and made everyone smile.

The 3 of them headed for a walk on the beach. They walked in the direction of Maggie's to avoid losing Teddy to Harry. Maggie was aware that the girls were coming to visit, Anna had a feeling she may have something up her sleeve. As they walked, the residents waved and other walkers greeted Anna by name.

"Wow," said Molly, "you really have settled in already!" Em sniffed, but Anna could see she had conceded this already.

As they approached Maggie's cottage, surprise, surprise, there she was on her deck.

"Couey," shouted Maggie as she beckoned them over. Teddy was first to run at full pelt towards Maggie. The 3 of them meandered over. "I have just made a jug of Pimm's, do you care to join me?" Anna didn't remember saying that Pimm's was Em's favorite tipple but she was glad either way.

The 3 of them settled on Maggie's luxurious deck with a glass of Pimm's each, perfectly dressed with ice, mint and fruit. Maggie also produced a plate of delicious sweet and savory nibbles. Em looked very at home, happily chatting with Maggie, enjoying the envious glances on the onlookers walking by.

Molly was lounging on a big fluffy rug on the floor with Barbara and Teddy, once in a while coming up to grab another handful of nibbles. Maggie took all 3 for a tour of her beach house, all three were impressed with the luxurious fittings and space this overgrown beach house gave. Molly loved the upstairs viewing platform stating, "I bet you see some great stuff from here!" She said, It really was a beautiful home.

They settled back down on the front deck enjoying the sunshine, as they finished off their Pimm's and Molly hoovered up the last of the nibbles. Maggie announced that she was going away for a couple of nights and needed a dog/house sitter. Much to Anna's surprise, Em enthusiastically offered herself for the job.

Maggie immediately stated, "You should bring your fiancé and enjoy a few days by the sea, make a little holiday of it." Em was delighted and Molly rolled her eyes with a knowing grin, she knew exactly what was going on here and didn't mind a bit. Molly loved her mum's new life and was glad she was happy. She also liked Maggie and she was happy that her mum had taken the plunge. Molly was also looking forward to future visits, she loved the ocean too.

The three of them waved goodbye to Maggie and meandered back to Anna's cottage. The girls relaxed on the sofa while Anna set about laying out the picnic platter. It was late afternoon and a chill had crept in so they decided to eat in the lounge. Anna lit the wood burner and laid the platter on the coffee table.

They chattered and laughed and watched the walkers on the beach and the waves ebb and flow. "I love it here, Mum," said Molly. Em nodded with a slight smile on her face. Maybe Maggie's invite had been enough to sway Emily.

As the afternoon started to move into evening, the girls bid their goodbyes with lots of hugs and kisses. Both had their sausage rolls packed up. Molly had hovered up all that was left of the picnic and packed it with her sausage rolls.

Anna stood and waved as she watched the car move out of sight. "Come on, Teddy, let's get in." The day had gone quite well.

Chapter 4
What Next

The weeks were flying by as Anna settled into her new life. She hadn't expected to settle into such a special community also. The move to the beach house had been more to escape the life she had found herself living in, everything else was an unexpected bonus.

With the time passing, came the fact that Anna needed to find an income; she didn't need to earn vast amounts, just enough to enable her to cover her daily expenses. Maggie was the obvious choice for some advice so she had texted her and a walk was planned for that day.

Maggie agreed to meet at Anna's, as Anna had promised Harry some home-made sausage rolls, so Anna would drop them off on the way by. Harry was happy to see them both. Teddy was already settled on his lap by the time the two of them reached Harry's deck.

Tea was offered and accepted and they chatted happily as the world went by. Harry had tucked into one of the sausage rolls and was making noises to show his approval. "You should sell these, Anna," Harry announced. "The walkers on the beach would love these!" They both glanced at Maggie at the same time who had raised her eyebrows and had a wry smile on her face.

Harry and Maggie both looked at each other and then back to Anna. "Would you like to have a look around my beach café next door," asked Harry. "It's a bit run down, but I think with some TLC, it would be a great venue to sell your sausage rolls from. I would love to see the café up and running again and I can't think of anyone else I would rather see running the old place."

Anna nodded eagerly. "Yes, please, I would love to." Now excited, that would be a bit of dream come true for Anna. Harry had received many offers on the café, but had always refused them, concerned by what the café would be turned into, he liked Anna and sensed she would have good intentions for the old place.

The three of them headed across to the café. It wasn't big, but then Anna only needed a small income. *It would take some work to get it up and running but it would be perfect,* thought Anna as she investigated every inch of the café as she set straight chairs, pepper pots and stands.

She turned towards Harry and Maggie, both were stood watching with great beams on their faces. The funny thing was, Anna hadn't even talked to Maggie that morning about finding an income, somehow, she simply knew.

Anna walked Maggie back to her cottage. Anna chatted away excited by the new prospect. Maggie was pleased for her and Harry, and very pleased that the beach café would be up and running again. Anna's head was full of excitement and ideas; never in her wildest dreams could she of expected her life to unfold in such a way.

She called her daughters in excitement. Em was not that impressed but wished her mother well; Molly was super excited and offered to help out in the holidays in exchange for board and lodgings. Harry had refused any rental payment. He simply asked that Anna looked after the utilities and upkeep, the only rent he wanted was lunch any day that the café was open, both parties agreed.

Anna could hardly sleep with excitement that night. She rose early and decided to take Teddy for a walk past the beach café, taking in her new vista and imagining her plans for the place. She wanted a larger deck, part of which would be covered. She planned to open Wednesday to Sunday, from 10 till 2, the café was all she could think about.

First, Anna needed to get all the legalities sorted. Maggie had said she would help with these as she worked on the board of the town council, surprise, surprise! Maggie had also offered to contact the carpenter who built her cottage. Anna was not able to complete any of the wood or building work herself. Anna only had a small budget to put towards the renovation.

Maggie had assured her that the builder lived locally and always offered favorable rates for work within the community and by the looks of Maggie's house, he did a good job. As Anna approached Harry's cottage, she could see Harry on his deck, he waved and beckoned her over. Teddy ran ahead as usual.

As she approached, Harry disappeared into his cottage and came out a couple of moments later, naturally Teddy followed him. As Anna approached his deck, he held out a key, it was the key to the café. "For you, my dear."

"Already?" Anna stated.

"No time like the present," stated Harry. Anna took the key as though it was a precious gift.

"Would you mind if I went over to the café now so I can start to establish a plan of action," asked Anna.

"The café is yours, Anna, come and go as you please," smiled Harry. He was looking forward to seeing the café come back to life, along with the comings and goings of the customers who would visit. The arrangement would benefit them all. He knew the locals would be very pleased to see it up and running again.

Anna walked next door to the café. She stood for a while in front of it, still not quite believing that this was going to be her place. Her own little café by the sea—a dream she never imagined would actually come true. She unlocked the café for the first time, pushing on the heavy creaking door to get it to open.

The café had a long counter across the back and a small working area behind this. The café had 4 tables, 2 four seaters and 2 two seaters, all with wonderful views out to sea. There was also plenty of room for walkers to get a takeaway from the counter without disturbing the seated guests.

The first thing needed was a good clean and a fresh coat of paint. Anna spent more than an hour in the café, tidying rubbish, setting things straight and just standing imagining what the café would be like. As she headed home, she waved to Harry who was stood on his deck smiling.

He would be very happy to see the café back up and running and he was glad it had given Anna purpose. He could tell she had been through a lot and Harry liked her.

That afternoon, Anna drove into Cromer for paint, cleaning products and other items for the café. She could not help but purchase a couple of driftwood boats she saw in the Garden House window, her favorite shop in Cromer which sold lots of wonderful arts and crafts. Once she had all the supplies she needed and had loaded them into the car, she popped to No1, a traditional fish and chip shop up on the cliff top overlooking the sea.

It used to be a rundown café which also sold ice cream, rock and all the usual seaside fair. Anna remembered her father buying her all manner of sweet treats from the big front display window, which would be open wide and serve as a counter to the street, tempting all the children and adults alike as they walked back to the car after a day on the beach.

Anna would often ask for one of the bright red candy dummies, with a yellow plastic circle set into it, threaded with a red ribbon you could hang around your neck and encased in shiny clear plastic sleave. These would hang from the top of the open display window, along with bags of candy floss which you could smell in the air along with hot donuts, rock and much, much more.

If they had a long car journey, Anna knew the large red dummy would keep her going all the way home.

This was back in the days when there was always a Punch and Judy show on the promenade in front on the beach, set up in a tall thin red and white striped tent. There would be a chalk board leaned up against it detailing the show times and price. Anna would plague her parents and eventually receive two shiny five pence pieces, enough for her and her big sister to attend.

They would sit on the sandy concrete in their swimming costumes, arriving early to get a good seat. The puppeteer would come around with a red velvet pouch fitted into a hoop on the end of a long stick, where the children would drop their pennies into before the show began. The parents would get to relax in peace on the beach as the children were mesmerized by the performance of Mr. punch and his slapstick antics, normally consisting of someone being hit with a stick.

Anna remembered there being a crocodile and Mr. Punch often falling foul of its sharp clapping teeth. Anna smiled as she thought of those times.

The old café had been closed for a while before it was bought by Galton Blackiston, a local chef who often featured on one of her favorite programs, Saturday Morning Kitchen. He had set up the fish and chip takeaway shop. A downstairs fish and chip restaurant and an upstairs fish restaurant, selling more refined and international dishes, all with amazing views over the ocean, beach and pier.

Anna purchased a fish supper to take home, along with a Jumbo sausage for Teddy. She was intending to get up early tomorrow to start cleaning and decorating the café. Anna still had to pinch herself. She was making her own decisions and nobody was there to look down their nose at her or question her choices. She had doubted herself and here she was steering her own ship and loving it!

The next morning, Anna practically jumped out of bed, had a swift breakfast and headed over to the café to make a start. She loaded the car and drove what was a few moments along the dune road behind the cottages and café, pulling into the parking space behind the café. Anna felt so excited, along with daunted about the amount of work the back of the café displayed.

Without a second thought, Anna was out of the car and unloaded, she set about scrubbing, cleaning and polishing. By mid-afternoon, the café was starting to take shape. The old sink sparkled and the thick wooden counted shone with the new application of beeswax and polish.

The heavy wooden tables and chairs had come up well too and added a look of lived in and loved. The windows were clean and showing off the amazing sea view and the two driftwood boats she had purchased were proudly placed on one of the windowsills. The start of many touches which would make the café a special place to be.

Anna purveyed the café with pride as Harry knocked on the door. Anna beckoned him in. After looking around for a few moments, Harry turned to Anna with tears in his eyes and thanked her. Before long, they were both in tears and hugging each other. Anna not only felt like part of a community but part of a family also.

As the afternoon drifted on, regulars on the beach popped their heads in to say how excited they were, asking for an opening date. Anna had been so swept up by the clean-up, she had yet to follow up all the legalities of opening a café. As much as she wanted to start painting and further progressing the café, tomorrow had to be an admin day.

A few days later, Anna had her food hygiene certificate and the local authority were due to inspect the premises to award her food hygiene rating. The oven had been cleaned and serviced and all the mains had been connected; Anna was ready for inspection. Just as Anna was about to take one last round of inspecting the café herself, she caught sight of something scurrying along the far side of the café.

Anna screamed and ran towards the door colliding with the person then coming through the door. As terrified of rats as Anna was, she jumped into the arms of the stranger at the door, practically scrambling up him and clinging around his neck. "Can I put you down somewhere you feel safe?"

"The beach, ten yards away," was all Anna could get out. "Please don't say you are the hygiene inspector."

"No, I'm glad to disappoint you, Maggie asked I call in about the deck."

On the beach ten yards away, Anna regained her composure without taking hers eyes off the café. Without any introduction Anna blurted out, "You have to help me, the local department of health are due any time now to inspect the café and…"

"There is a rat in there, which you are terrified of," relayed the stranger, who without hesitation headed into the café. After lots of banging and commotion, she saw the big black rat propel itself out of the café door at speed and up into the dunes. Anna let out a scream and jumped back further, just as terrified.

The stranger laughed at her as she shuddered and jumped about shaking herself as if the rat had just been thrown at her. Anna stopped her repelled rat dance and glared at him, which seemed to make him laugh further, which annoyed Anna further.

The stranger went back Into the café and came out a few moments later. "All clear," he stated.

"Are you sure," shouted Anna.

"Yep." Anna headed back into the café.

"Thank you," she said clasping and shaking his hand. "I'm Anna."

"I figured. I'm…" but before he could finish there was a knock at the door, it was the inspector. "I'll pop back tomorrow," said the stranger and headed out as Anna welcomed the inspector in, firmly shutting the café door.

The inspection went well, and Anna received a five-star award. The inspector was none the wiser of the recent unwelcome visitor. As soon as the inspector was gone, Anna closed up and headed home. She would bring Teddy with her tomorrow and contact a pest controller as soon as she got home.

The next morning, Anna met the pest controller at the café, heaving a sigh of relief as she saw his van parked outside the café as she pulled up. She gave him the keys and he gave her a knowing smile as he headed into the café. Anna took Teddy onto the beach in front of the café.

After what Anna felt was a safe period, she headed towards the café, the stranger from yesterday was also there, chatting with the pest controller; they clearly knew each other. Both men turned towards Anna and smiled as she approached.

"The café is all clear, there are a couple of areas that could give access to rodents, but I have discussed this with Adam (motioning towards the stranger) and he will secure these. I've added traps in and around the building. I will call back in a week to check these and relay if required."

"Rats don't like movement so you being here will act as a deterrent, keep your rubbish tidy and you shouldn't have a problem." Anna thanked the man and he nodded his goodbye.

Anna turned to the stranger and held out her hand. "Adam, I believe?" Adam shook her hand and smiled.

"A very different greeting to yesterday," stated Adam with a smile. "Women are always jumping into my arms when I meet them, I'm used to it," he stated dryly with a smile. "I'm just glad it was me and not the inspector. How did it go?"

"Well," said Anna, "five stars."

"That's great, I'm glad for you. Everything happens for a reason and at least you will have that covered before you open up to the public." Anna nodded and smiled. "Maggie asked me to pop over about the deck and any other jobs you might want doing before you open, including the potential rodent access points."

"Brilliant," said Anna as she started to explain what she wanted for the deck. They chatted happily for about an hour about Anna's ideas and Adam offered his own. The two of them were on the same wavelength, both excited by what the café could offer the beach walkers and the community around.

"It's going to be great, Anna, I can't wait to see the old café open again. I can remember coming here as a child. I was worried it was going to be converted to another residence and that I might be asked to do it, so I'm honored to be part of bringing this lovely old lady back to life."

Anna liked Adam, he set about the rodent access and stated measuring up for the new deck. Anna was glad to have him around. Teddy also liked Adam, following him around and getting his nose into any spot Adam did. Anna would hear periodic laughs from Adam as Teddy got in close and licked his ear, which made Anna smile.

Anna started painting the café; a combination of soft white, a muted duck egg green and a light blue, along with taupe and grey. She wanted the café to be a welcoming, warn and calm place to enjoy the views and catch up with friends. She planned to replace one of the small tables with a comfy sofa and coffee table.

She was intending on having a wood burning stove installed inside and possibly one on the covered part of the deck. She had also spoken to Adam about having a hanging sofa swing on the deck which she could add comfortable cushioning to. Adam headed off to collect some of the timber he needed for the deck and restoration of the café.

He liked Anna and her plans; he would enjoy the restoration and seeing the café come to life. He also had a soft spot for Teddy. He had lost his dog a couple of years ago and missed having a dog around.

Anna was still painting as Adam returned with the timber and made a start on the deck. Anna made them bacon sandwiches and cups of tea. She enjoyed using the café kitchen, it had a good feel about it. These would be the first of many sandwiches and teas she would make.

Anna planned a simple menu of bacon, cheese, and of course Cromer crab sandwiches. She would have her home-made sausage rolls available and the cake of the day. She was so looking forward to trying out the café oven. She had ordered herself a Kitchen-Aid in pistachio green for making the cakes, along with other kitchen items she would need.

That evening, she would decide on and order the cutlery, plates and cups. It was so exciting, she felt like a child at Christmas. As late afternoon hit, Anna took two cool bottles of beer out of the café fridge; she had already stocked the café with a few essentials which she had brought along that morning. She loved the fact that the café was already coming into its own.

She walked out onto the deck with the two beers. "Wow!" Anna exclaimed. Adam had cracked on with the deck, she handed a beer to Adam.

"Perfect, thank you," he said, Anna smiled.

"It's looking amazing already," said Anna.

"As is the interior," stated Adam. "It's going to be an amazing place. The community needs it and it's good to know that Harry will have company and be well fed," he said with a smile as he clinked his beer bottle against Anna's.

Anna smiled up at him too. *She liked being around Adam*, she thought, they both stood leaning against the café looking out to sea It was a beautiful end to a beautiful day.

Chapter 5
The Café Opens

Anna had been flat out for several weeks now and the café was ready. It was Saturday and Anna was having a celebration to thank all those involved in the opening of the café. The official opening of the café due on the following Wednesday.

Anna had not published the opening, but she had put a simple poster in the window stating when it would open and the times, mainly because Anna was having to repeat herself to all the passes-by that asked. She also did not want to attract too many on her first few days as she settled into a routine with the café and established the demand for the offerings she had.

The café looked amazing. Adam had done an fantastic job on the deck, swinging chair and chalk board, along with converting part of the main frontal banister into a storage bench and storage ottomans along the front wall which also doubled as seats. He had added small wooden shaped shelf boxes along the inside and outside of the café to house objects, tea-lights and anything else that needed a home.

Adam had built her a dog station where fresh water could be tapped into water bowls and housed 2 glass jars of dog biscuits in the circular holes Adam had cut into the top. There were also doggy blankets for wet or cold dogs, beside this was a wicker basket of blankets for the dog's human companions on colder days.

There was an outside log burner, with a stash of logs underneath. Adam had produced small chalk boards with rope hangers attached to enable anna to write information on for her guests, the boards were hung on or beside the different elements such as 'human blankets' and 'feel free to stock the fire with logs'.

He had hung festoon light all around the front and sides of the café which Anna could turn on from the inside, a guiding and magical sight on dull days or on evening celebrations such as this evening.

Anna was laying on a hog roast on the beach beside the café, along with a selection of quiches, crab canapés and sausage rolls inside the café. Earlier that week, while chatting with Harry and Maggie about what to serve, Harry had produced a large black pit BBQ which wouldn't look out of place in The Deep South USA, but Harry promised it did the job.

Adam had taken on the job of pit master. He had fresh rolls and apple sauce to serve with the pulled pork, leaving Anna free to cover everything else. It also meant that any passes by and potential future customers could be involved in the celebration as there would be plenty to go around.

Maggie arrived early to help Anna set up. Maggie brought Pimm's, Prosecco and lemonade. There was plenty of ice in the freezer and beer in the fridge. Anna had nuts, nibbles, cocktail sausage rolls and Cromer Crab canapés all plated up, placed and covered ready for the guest's arrival. Adam had the hog well on the way. He had set up earlier and lit the roast as the hog would take several hours to cook.

Once ready, the three friends sat on the new deck and relaxed with a cool beer, chatting happily watching the waives as the first guests started to arrive, before long the café was alive with the sound of conversation and laughter. Anna jumped up and turned on the festoon light which brought a round of applause. "I declare the Beach Café open!"

Everyone cheered and clinked glasses, the pest controller, Harry, the owners of Anna's cottage, her daughters and partners and many others involved in the set-up, supply and opening of Anna's café; including the Davies family who caught and supplied the Cromer Crabs were in attendance, enjoying the food and company.

The hog roast was a roaring success as were the sausage rolls and crab canapés. A log pit had been dug into the sand and lit with logs collected by all the guests. The celebrations went on long into the evening without the worry of disturbing the neighbors as they had all been invited and attended.

Anna sat by the fire looking around at the happy faces of her new friends, as the moonlight glistened on the gently rolling waves, the evening couldn't have gone any better. As Anna moved her gaze back from the waves to the friends around the camp fire, she locked eyes with Adam who was sat watching her. They held each other's gaze for a moment until Adam mouthed, "Well done!"

Anna beamed back at him as she felt tears of pride and happiness well within her.

Anna woke late the next morning with a slightly delicate head. After a few cups of tea, Anna and Teddy headed to the café to assess the damage. Her guests had been kind and disposed of their rubbish correctly. Anna had done a quick clean round last night to avoid leaving out anything which could attract vermin and the hog roaster had been safely locked up, in the vermin proof metal shed behind the café.

All Anna needed to do was a quick clean round, ready for tomorrow's deliveries to stock and prepare the café for the opening on Wednesday. Anna locked up and headed back to the cottage for a lazy afternoon in the cottage watching the waves, ready for the busy week ahead.

Anna set off for the café early the next day with Teddy. The sausage meat was delivered by the local butcher; the final catering supplies arrived and a local artisan ice-cream producer arrived with ice-creams and lollies. The drinks order was delivered last week and once all the fresh produce was packed away, Anna started on the cakes and sausage rolls.

She would make enough sausage rolls for the week and cook them off fresh each morning or as needed. Anna made the cakes ready for icing the next day, made a crab quiche and gave the café another clean; she set up the counter and tables for the next day. The next morning, her intention was to cook off the sausage rolls, make up some sandwiches and put the coffee on.

She didn't have room for a fancy coffee maker so had found a local producer who roasted and ground his own beans and would deliver a regular supply for her coffee machine, which all her tasters have given the thumbs up to. The doors would open at 10am the next morning. Maggie had offered to help in case she had a rush on opening day and while she found her feet.

Anna was ready, she looked around her and couldn't quite believe how far she had come. The café looked stunning!

Anna gazed at the waves through the café window, lost in her thoughts as Adam walked onto the deck. Anna turned and smiled at him as Teddy jumped up and down at the door eager to get to Adam. Anna opened the door and welcomed him in, "Wow," said Adam. "It looks amazing!"

"Thanks," she smiled. "Beer?"

"Yes, please, here I brought this for you." It was a driftwood sign. 'The Café on the Beach' was etched into the smooth driftwood. Tears welled in Anna's eyes as she thanked Adam and gave him a quick hug.

"It's perfect," she told him. Anna collected the beers as Adam hung the sign, after they both admired it for a while, they sat on the hanging sofa on the deck, gently swinging, chatting and watching the waives.

The next morning, Anna was finishing setting up the counter as Maggie walked in. The smell of hot sausage rolls and fresh coffee hit her. "If it tastes anything like it smells, you are going to have some very happy customers," exclaimed Maggie.

Teddy greeted Maggie with excitement, the café was dog friendly, but Teddy wasn't allowed behind the bar, much to his distain; each time Anna ushered him back as he inched his nose over the threshold again! Anna had cooked off bacon which was keeping warm in the chafing dish and Maggie was finishing buttering the rolls, they were ready.

As Anna walked over to the café door and flipped the driftwood sign to open (another gift from Adam). Anna suddenly felt nervous. She looked to Maggie who gave her a reassuring beam, she took a deep breath and opened the door, there was already a small group waiting for the café to open. Within an hour, the café and outside area were full.

The service had gone very smoothly due to all the preparations and set up of the café. Guests could help themselves to a tray, add cold drinks, crisps and snacks and pay for these at the counter while ordering and waiting for any hot food and drinks to be added, along with any cutlery which Anna would add to their trays. As one table left, Maggie would give it a quick clean and another group of guests would fill it.

Morning turned into lunch and the guest of honor arrived for his lunch. Harry sat and chatted with the other quests, many of which knew him. The café buzzed with chat and laughter. As the last guests left just after 2pm, Anna flipped the sign and closed the door.

Leaning against it, "Phew," she exclaimed as she looked to Maggie. The four hours had gone in the blink of an eye. "Prosecco?" Anna asked, of course Maggie agreed.

As they sat and relaxed on the swing seat sipping their prosecco, apologizing to the numerous walkers who asked if they were open, Adam turned up, again with another much larger driftwood sign. This one sporting two stakes which could be pushed into the sand. "What does this one say?" Anna asked.

Adam turned the sign round, on it in large letters, hung on two hooks was 'Sorry, we are closed', followed by the opening times. The three of them laughed as Adam anchored the sign close enough to be associated with the café but far away enough to give those in the café some privacy. Anna opened her mouth to ask Adam if he would like a beer, before she could Adam put up his hand.

"I'll get it." The three of them relaxed in the afternoon sun while Anna and Maggie gave Adam the low down on how the café's first day had gone. Takings were good and although, she knew winter would be slower, Anna knew this was a viable way for her to support herself in her new life. Maggie would help her for the rest of this week, then Anna would go it alone.

She was quite confident that with the correct preparation, she would manage well. The customers seemed happy to wait if there was a que and it was small enough for her to cope. She would need to make more sausage rolls and she would have some packaged and ready to go on the counter and in the self-service chiller along with Cromer crab and other assorted sandwiches and small plates, so guests could self-serve or purchase to take home.

Anna packed up, cleaned down the café and headed home. She fell asleep on the sofa with Teddy snuggled beside her.

The weeks flew by as Anna settled into her new routine. She already knew most of her regulars by name. Anna had a good stack of logs delivered ready for the winter, by another local Maggie knew and Adam had built her a log store. Anna's days were not as busy now as the initial rush had died down and autumn approached.

She enjoyed running the café and chatting with her regulars who were quickly becoming friends. The beach was not well known, other than by regulars so the café would never be overrun by holiday makers. The beach itself was quite sheltered from the onslaught of the waves along the Norfolk coast, partly because of its makeup and because of the sea defenses paid for by the local residents, headed and organized by Maggie of course.

Anna was not sure what winter would bring, but she was sure all would be well. As the weather turned, the café turned out to be a warm haven for walkers to grab a hot drink or mug of soup, which Anna had started making freshly each morning. Anna loved her café and all the regulars who popped in. Anna grew closer to Harry as he gave his pearls of wisdom over his lunch each day.

He would also potter around the café clearing the tables and helping out with minor tasks. Harry seemed to enjoy his new role as Maître D, along with the company of Anna and the other guests, so she was happy for Harry to retain his daily routine. Anna would see him beam with pride as he relayed the history of the café to new customers.

The café had become a popular place to visit within the community and her customers would regularly thank her for bringing it back to life, Anna could never have dreamt she would become an important part of the community and she felt very settled and welcomed.

Chapter 6
It's the Most Wonderful
Time of the Year

Anna loved Christmas; it was by far her favorite time of year. It was mid-November and Anna was deep into preparations for the festive period. The café was still ticking over nicely even now, the locals still walked the beach.

On days where the weather was particularly bad, Anna would be slower but some customers would specifically come to the café on those days so they could enjoy the coastal views from the cozy comfort of the café.

Anna would also use the time to stock up on her sausage rolls and stash them unbaked in the freezer, especially as she was getting orders for them to cook at home from frozen, along with ready to eat sausage rolls for parties and for the Christmas period. Anna loved being in the café.

It was like a home from home, where friends joined her. Sometimes Anna would have a cup of tea and sit and chat with the locals or simply get lost in her thoughts mesmerized by the waves and the weather fronts coming and going, the café with the warm glow from the wood burner was Anna thought, possibly the most wonderful place in the world.

Anna had ordered 3 Christmas trees this year—a small one for inside the café, a large potted one for outside the café and one for her cottage. The two for the café were arriving today. Anna had asked Adam if he could collect and deliver the trees in his pick-up.

She hadn't seen Adam in what felt like ages as he had been working away and she had to admit that she had missed him. Anna had closed at 2pm as usual and completed her clean down. Adam was due around 3pm. Anna was decorating the café as Adam arrived. As he walked in Anna couldn't help but run in for a hug.

Adam stood with open arms and scooped her up for a bear hug. It was a hug of long lost friends but Anna couldn't help but rest her head on Adam's powerful shoulders and enjoy the hug which probably went on longer than it should. He smelt like a clean man with a hint of Christmas tree. As Adam placed her back on her feet, Anna stated, "You smell like a Christmas tree."

"That's because I have been wrestling with your extraordinarily large Christmas trees!"

"My trees!" Anna exclaimed jumping and clapping like an excited child. They both made their way outside.

It was indeed a big tree! Anna took the top of the tree while Adam wrestled with the large heavy pot. They wrestled the tree to the side of the café hindered by their own laughter, as Adam was repeatedly swallowed up by the tree. They were both still laughing when the tree was in place.

Anna had tears running down her face as she had been laughing so much. The sight of the large figure becoming one with the tree and the sounds coming from within the tree just heightened Anna's laughter, causing her to loose strength and drop the tree, causing Adam to disappear further into the tree, causing Anna to drop to her knees in hysterics.

Adam was smiling at Anna as she kept bursting into fits of giggles as she recalled the antics. Once Anna had finally composed herself, they made their way inside the café and they both sat at one of the tables with a warming glass of mulled cider. They were looking out at the waves and admiring the new tree.

Adam had helped Anna so much over the last few months and she had been wondering how to thank him. "Can I cook you dinner one night in the café as a thank you for all your help, Adam?" Anna asked.

"I would be honored, Anna, but you don't need to. You have been a real tonic after the last few difficult years, but as I enjoy your company as much as I enjoy your food. I accept, thank you."

Anna clapped her hands to her chest. "Excellent," she exclaimed.

Anna decorated the café over the next few days and set up a bain-marie to serve warm mulled wine and cider which filled the café with wonderful Christmassy scents. She also had hot chocolate spiced with cinnamon, which she would decorate with whipped cream, marsh mellows and top with a candy cane; this went down well with children and adults alike.

Anna was looking forward to having Adam over for a meal. They had decided on Sunday as Adam had finished work for the Christmas period and this was the end of the working week for Anna, so they could relax into the evening without worry about work the next day. She had been mulling over what to cook.

She settled on slow roast lamb shanks with a dauphinoise potatoes and a red current gravy reduction from the cooking juices served with minted peas and green vegetables and red cabbage. For dessert, she would make brandy snap baskets; she would coat the inside will dark chocolate and fill with clotted chattily cream and fresh berries.

Anna arrived at the café on Sunday excited. She put the lamb shanks on to slow cook after she had baked off the day's sausage rolls. She set up the café as normal and welcomed her first regulars. Many locals had made a visit to the café as part of their routine; some would be there at 10am on the dot with their paper in hand and sit in the exact same chair and order the same items each day.

Anna would already be preparing their order as she saw them come up the beach. The regulars kept the café ticking over through the winter. She would also get a lot of dog walkers visit for the first time on the recommendation of friends, delighting in the secret gem they found at the beach café, especially since the decorations and the outside tree had gone up.

Anna had decorated the tree with warm twinkling lights with gold and silver baubles. Inside was like a twinkling grotto; the log fire and sea views all made it a very magical place to be.

As the day went on, Anna prepared for the meal she had planned with Adam, but she did have a niggling doubt that she was inviting in more than she wanted. She did not want another relationship after splitting from 20 years of marriage. She liked her freedom and the life she had.

She shook the feeling off. She had done the same for Maggie on many occasions to thank her for all her help, why should this be any different? Anna shrugged of the thoughts swirling in her head and set about cleaning down the café after the last guest left.

Anna rearranged the café so that the table they would dine at was close to the fire with sight of the tree outside and the moonlit ocean. The lamb was perfect, falling off the bone and resting while Anna got the reduction going in the pan. She cooked and blanched the green veg and would put them into a warm oven for holding before Adam arrived.

The red cabbage had been cooked slowly with apple and spices and the potatoes were in, as Anna finished off the desert and set it in the fridge. An hour later, everything was ready and keeping warm in the oven. Anna had laid the table with a cloth and lit candles, with time to spare.

The evening was clear and chilly outside. The moon was bright and its reflection lead a light path on the ocean, which flickered as the waves caught it. As Anna watched through the window mesmerized, Adam approached the café from the beach; he had walked from his home. Anna hadn't noticed him as he stopped in his tracks.

Anna was framed by the candlelight and the glow from the fire. The sight of Anna had taken Adam's breath away. He knew he had feelings for Anna but could tell she was still finding herself after her marriage break-up, so he had kept his distance. Seeing Anna looking out to the ocean that evening was going to make it hard for Adam to keep his distance.

Adam strode up the steps to the front on the café, Anna turned and welcomed him in. Anna's heart skipped a beat as Adam walked through the door. She hadn't seen him dressed smart. He wore smart dark blue jeans and a white shirt, a mid-brown blazer, checked scarf and polished brown shoes, a little worse for the sand. Adam kissed Anna on the cheek and handed her a bunch of white and lime green flowers.

Anna thought she might faint. She busied herself putting the flowers in water as she composed herself. "Wine or beer?" She asked Adam; they both started with a beer.

"It looks magical, Anna." *As do you,* thought Adam.

"Thanks, I love this place," she said looking around the café she had grown to love. As she looked back, Adam was watching her and their eyes locked. "Dinner," said Anna, Adam took this as a sign to take it slow. He didn't mind, Anna was worth waiting for, he enjoyed her company and he was in no hurry himself.

The dinner went well. Adam was impressed and cleaned his plate. They chattered and laughed, enjoying the ambiance of their private dining room. Adam kept the wood burner stocked as Anna served up the meal. With the plates cleared, they both sat on the sofa watching the moon across the water and the lights on the tree sway and twinkle in the breeze.

"So, Adam, what's your story? You said you had a couple of rough years. Do you care to enlighten me with the history of Adam? I feel I know so little about you."

Adam sighed, he had known this was coming and he felt if he wanted to get to know Anna better, he would have to open up himself. Adam went on to explain how he too had lost both his parents in the last few years. He was happily married and had wanted children but his wife hadn't, so he had respected her wishes and accepted that they would not start a family, much to his dismay.

After his parents died, he launched himself into work as a way of coping with his loss, working away a lot, which he felt had affected his marriage. One Friday, 2 years ago, he had come home to find his wife gone, all that she owned had been moved out and a note left stating she had met someone else and that she was sorry.

That was it, he hadn't seen or heard from her since. He had no idea where she was or who she was with; he had asked around and nobody had a clue. He had tried to phone her on numerous occasions and left dozens of messages, eventually the number became unavailable, that was it.

It had hit him hard and he again concentrated on his work as he had no one else to focus on. He lost touch with his close friends and didn't return calls. Then one night in a London bar in early December, a guy fronted up to him and he snapped. He couldn't even remember what happened, but after a night in the cell, he decided to get help.

He took a month off and got some counselling. He re-connected with his friends and the community and reduced his workload, doing more local work for individuals rather than big business and he shifted his focus from making money to enriching his and his customer lives. Anna had stayed quiet throughout the time Adam spoke.

He now looked up at her and she could see the pain in his eyes. Anna hugged him, in a way a mother would hug a child; she drew his head into the nape of her neck and held him close.

The pair shut up the café and Adam walked Anna back to her cottage. Anna linked her arm into Adam's feeling slightly brave from all the wine. She also felt the sadness he held and wanted to fix it. It felt nice to be close to him, she had not had this sort of closeness with her husband for many years and she realized she had missed it.

Adam too liked the closeness of Anna and hoped he could get closer to her over the festive break. The pair walked slowly along the beach chatting and laughing about the tree installation and how they had first met. Anna cringed at the thought of jumping into the arms of a complete stranger but laughed at the same time.

"I knew then that I wanted to spend time with you," said Adam.

"Did you?" Anna asked as she stopped to look at him under the moonlight, without knowing they kissed.

Anna softened to the thought of another man in her life that evening. Their experiences of life over the last few years was different, but also paralleled with a similarity. They had both suffered loss and rejection, they had also both decided to change the course of their lives for the better. They both felt a renewed connection with each other.

Chapter 7

The next morning, Molly was arriving to stay for the Christmas break. Anna intended to serve Christmas dinner in the café as her cottage was so tiny and didn't have the facilities of the café, nor the view or ambiance. She could prep the day before and walk over along the beach with the girls and Teddy after the present opening.

She also wanted to make sure all her new found friends were welcomed. Christmas Day was special and a day to be with loved ones. Anna didn't know if Maggie and Adam had any plans for the big day, so they were on the guest list.

Anna welcomed Molly as she arrived and left her to settle in as she headed over to open up the café. Later, Molly arrived and helped Anna in the café. They wandered back to the cottage later that afternoon enjoying the late winter sunshine and chatted merrily, waving to the other residents as they went.

Later, they wandered over to Maggie's and drank a cool glass of prosecco as they watched the world go by through the windows at the front of the beach house, cozy from the heat of the log burner. While there, Anna asked Maggie about Christmas dinner. "What a fabulous idea," replied Maggie.

"But I insist on hosting. My son and his wife are coming, it would be much more fun with a larger group. We can invite

Harry and Adam, as I'm sure they don't have plans," smiled Maggie. "I have more than enough room here and I insist, it would be a busman's holiday for you to host and I already have everything planned. I just need to up the numbers, how exciting," exclaimed Maggie clapping her hands together, at the thought of a big Christmas get together.

"I already have a private chef booked in and I am now looking forward to playing the hostess with the mostess," beamed Maggie. Anna agreed happily, she knew there was no changing Maggie's mind. She had also seen how excited Maggie had become at the thought of hosting. It would be a nice change not to cook and she was pleased Adam and Harry would be invited.

It would be a good Christmas; more like the family Christmases she remembered as a child. Anna had 4 sisters so Christmas had always been a busy affair. She hoped Harry and Adam would accept the invitation.

A few days later while setting up the café, Anna couldn't stop thinking about Adam's words the other evening. Just at that moment, Adam walked into the café, causing Anna to jump. "Morning, Anna, sorry I didn't mean to startle you," said Adam with a smile.

"Good morning," she smiled pleased to see him. "Can I get you something to drink?"

"A tea would be lovely, thank you," Anna busied herself making the tea and took it over to Adam. "So, to what do I owe this pleasure?" Anna asked.

"Well, I thought it was time I cooked for you, so I wanted to know if you would like to come to me for dinner?"

"That's the second invite in a week," stated Anna. Adam raised his eyebrows. "Maggie, Christmas day?"

"Ah yes, I have an invite too. She said she had invited you. She does throw an amazing bash; you will enjoy it, as will I and I am glad you are coming." They agreed that coming Sunday for the meal at Adam's. She didn't even know where he lived. "5 doors down from Maggie," replied Adam. Of course it would be thought Anna.

After locking up the café on Sunday, she walked back to the cottage with Molly and Teddy. "Are you nervous about your date tonight?" Molly asked.

"It's not a date, Molly, just a meal with a friend. Adam has been good to me and I like his company."

"A romantic candlelit dinner for two, just friends," teased Molly as she skipped around the beach singing, "love is in the air, everywhere I look around," while Teddy jumped up at her barking, thinking she was in distress. Anna smiled; she didn't mind Molly teasing her and she was glad Molly had taken the meal in good spirits, not that it was a date or anything!

Anna took a while to decide what to wear then went for simple smart jeans, blouse and jacket. She took some chilled English sparkling wine and headed towards Adam's along the beach. Molly had asked if Teddy could stay with her to keep her company. As she passed Maggie's, she got a wave.

She would normally get beckoned over, but naturally, Maggie knew the score and with a smile and a wave, returned inside. Was there anything that woman didn't know about thought Anna with a smile. Anna felt quite nervous, although she had said it was not a date, she knew that she was fooling herself somewhat.

Anna counted 5 cottages down from Maggie's. Adam's cottage was similar to Maggie's but it looked more manly. The woodwork was scorched black, a way of preserving the timber, it seemed to float off the ground somewhat and it had a second deck to the first floor. She caught sight of Adam on the balcony who waved a greeting before heading down to appear on the deck leading to the beach.

"Welcome," he greeted her as she approached. He took and thanked her for the wine and offered a glass. Anna followed him inside, the inside decor was more manly also with dark wood, glass and deep leather furnishing; it was simple but elegantly done. "I'll give you a tour," said Adam as he noticed her looking around.

On the ground floor was a small but comfortable entrance room with a couple of comfy chairs and a small bar with sink and glass storage integrated into it, enabling Adam to prepare refreshments for the lower deck. This lead to a hallway with 3 bedrooms and a front door and stairs up. "Wow," exclaimed Anna as she reached the first floor. "This is stunning, Adam!"

"Thank you, welcome to my haven." The upstairs was open plan, it had a large loft style feel to it, a kitchen to the back and a long island with gleaming black breakfast bar and to the front were comfortable sofas and chairs laid out to enable all to enjoy the view out to sea. In the corner was a back fireplace which seemed to hang from the ceiling and bulb out at the bottom while floating above the ground.

The sofas varied in subtle checks of grey, green and a muted red. they looked very expensive and exquisitely upholstered; it made Anna's cottage look ramshackle. The first floor balcony was deep and sheltered and had large comfortable chairs surrounding a sturdy coffee table. "Stunning, Adam, truly stunning."

"Thanks," said Adam as he appeared on the balcony with the wine. They sat and looked out to sea.

"Great view too."

"Indeed," said Adam. "Up here I can sit and admire the ocean without the fear or being disturbed. After my parents died and Sarah left, I realized eventually, that the one thing I needed most was space and time with my own thoughts; here I have that."

Adam served up a delicious lasagna and a fresh salad. "Playing it safe," said Adam as Anna made noises signifying it was good. "Plus I wanted to spend time with you, not the kitchen."

The evening was warm for the time of year so they sat on the balcony after dinner, enjoying the sound of the waves, both of them looked into the waves. "I never tire of the sight of the sea," said Adam.

"My thoughts exactly," agreed Anna. As the evening chill set in, they retired to the living room and Adam lit the fire, both of them took an arm chair option that sat closest to the fire.

"How are you finding living in our little community, it must be very different to your previous set up?" What Adam was really asking was how is single life?

"Good, I love it, everything about it. I wish I had done it sooner," replied Anna.

"Do you miss your husband?"

"No, not at all. Sometimes I feel sad that the relationship hadn't worked out because we were together for so long, but I'm glad I realized when I did. What about you, how are you?" Anna asked.

"Similar, however I have been happier since you arrived," added Adam. Anna smiled and did not look up. she didn't know how to react so Adam did it for her. "Shall I walk you home?"

"That would be lovely," replied Anna.

They walked and chatted as the moon shone bright on the calm sea that night. Adam had offered his elbow and Anna had accepted tucking her arm through his. She wondered if Maggie would see them walk by; she suspected she would! Anna enjoyed walking with Adam on the beach. They seemed to talk about something and nothing, just enjoying each other's company.

Again something she hadn't done with her husband for many years and it was only now, that she was really realizing what she had missed for far too long. The void of love that was their marriage had just existed for years, without Anna even realizing that their marriage been a lost cause for a long time until now.

Her husband had loved her like an old shirt, but he had not been in love with her and she had felt that, but stayed for the good of the children and for the safeness of the routine.

As the two of them arrived at Anna's cottage. They both knew this was a moment when an accepting embrace could occur, in the darkness, an allowance, not an acceptance of days going forward, just an allowance. They stood in the moonlight with the sound of the sea gently crashing against the shore and then pulling back out.

Adam looked at Anna and Anna smiled back. As Adam moved to kiss Anna, Anna gently entwined her hands into his coat lapels and they kissed. A communication that both of them understood and lingered in.

Adam stayed and watched to make sure Anna was safely inside before he walked home along the shore, happy with the sound of the door lock clicking, only just heard above the waves. He walked along the shore happy in his thoughts, not realizing he and Anna were being watched.

Christmas Eve arrived. Anna decided to close the café for the week leading up to Christmas as everyone would be busy preparing. She would open up on boxing day for the walkers and had invited her family over for a late afternoon gathering. Anna loved Christmas, so having the week leading up free was a joy, especially as she didn't need to worry about cooking on the big day.

The cottage was decorated and Anna had made personalized Christmas crackers for each guest on Christmas day, the only thing Maggie had agreed she could bring.

Anna had pastries for the morning and Bucks Fizz, along with a pile of presents waiting to be opened. She no longer had to hide them and get them out late on Christmas Eve, as her children were old enough now to know that Father Christmas was actually Mum. In Anna's mind, Father Christmas still existed.

She believed that he left a present for everyone under the tree, you just didn't know which one, and this is what she told her children, even now. Each day, Anna would purchase and wrap another gift or two and add them to the pile. She always gave Teddy a new bed each Christmas amongst other things, now wrapped and under the tree.

Anna loved having the time to choose gifts for her family and wrap them by the wood burning stove while watching the waves. She had made a trip to Norwich with a long list, all now wrapped and she had also shopped online for gifts. Her eldest daughter loved Jo Malone Candles and Chanel makeup; Molly loved anything she was given, especially if it involved something she could eat or snuggle in.

Emily arrived on Christmas Eve. the three of them settled in for a Christmas Eve buffet in their new Christmas Eve pajamas, an annual tradition. They watched Christmas movies and chatted excitedly, periodically picking at morsels from the buffet. Anna had also been slowly purchasing the traditional Christmas chocolate selection, which had to include Quality Street, Roses, Matchmakers Terry's Chocolate Orange and After Eights to name a few.

As Anna didn't have the expense of the Christmas day lunch, she was able to spend a little more on the buffet and Christmas Chocolates. Christmas Eve was the night the girls could open the chocolates and they drank mulled wine, slowly blipping in a pan on the hob. The cottage was picture perfect with all the festive decorations Anna had added.

The tree lights glistened and the pile of presents beneath it, promised the unknown excitement that the opening would bring the following morning.

On Christmas morning, the first thing Anna did was open the curtains. She never tired of seeing the ocean in the morning, and seeing it on Christmas morning was extra special. She had never seen the sea on Christmas day and so she stood and watched the waves roll. The odd walkers wondered by some with festive hats on and dogs with Christmas bow ties and coats, the odd one sported reindeer horns.

Anna loved Christmas! By the time the girls came down, Anna had restocked the wood burner with new logs and had the pastries in the oven. Tea was poured and Bucks Fizz, Anna had popped a couple of sausages in for Teddy. The radio was on playing Christmas songs and a Christmas movie was playing on the TV.

Molly and Em relaxed on the sofa, sometimes watching the TV, sometimes the fire and sometimes the beach. Molly on the chair by the window, as usual bursting into giggles of delight at any mishaps she observed on the beach. She was particularly amused as a very enthusiastic Great Dane, bombed over to its owner and took his legs completely from underneath him, momentarily leaving him airborne before gravity dumped him onto the wet sand in an undignified pile.

Molly burst out laughing as she relayed the incident, between bouts of laughter. "That's made my day," she trailed off sounding winded from her observations and reaction. Molly's reactions always made Em and Anna smile, as they exchanged a knowing glance.

Once they all had pastries, tea and Bucks Fizz, they sat down to open presents. Teddy sat proudly in his new bed chewing on a new chew. All three girls were delighted with the presents they received and enjoyed seeing each other open their gifts. Anna couldn't have asked for a more perfect morning and thought she would always want to wake up beside the sea on Christmas morning, with a log fire burning.

Anna smiled at the sight of her two daughters chatting and laughing. She was worried how this first Christmas would be without their father. She was glad they were going to Maggie's; she thought it would be good for everyone to celebrate as a larger group, taking the focus away from the fact that their father was missing from this Christmas celebration and Anna was looking forward to it. It was a nice change not to be busy cooking on Christmas day.

After the gift opening was finished and breakfast cleared, the three of them took Teddy for a walk on the beach before getting ready to head over to Maggie's for lunch. All of the girls had dressed up for lunch. All had a new top and jewelry to wear. Em also had tried out some of her new make-up, taking the longest to get ready.

The three girls headed along the beach to Maggie's. On arrival, they were all greeted like long lost friends. Maggie's house looked tastefully amazing with fresh green garlands, wreaths, candle decorations and festive deer figurines, amongst many special touches around the house and outside decking, with twinkling warm lights adorning every corner.

Everyone was in a festive and cheerful mood. It was one of those days you would remember forever. There was a happy vibe throughout the house and happy laughter and chat could be heard all around.

Dinner was served around Maggie's large oval table which easily sat all eight quests, who included Anna and the girls, Maggie, her son and his wife, Harry and Adam. Champagne was served in ornate flutes and the private chef, effortlessly produced beautiful food, served by the waiter, laid in the center of the table in beautiful serving bowls with lids and vegetable platters.

The main event were the individual beef and vegetable wellingtons and a carved Turkey. For afters, there was Christmas puddings and a chocolate log served with clotted cream and raspberries. Freshly ground Irish coffees were served after with handmade chocolate and rum truffles.

The hired waiter cleared the table as the friends chatted over their coffees and then Anna brought out the large crackers she had made up, each adorned with the guests names. Inside were the usual hats and jokes along with gifts especially chosen for the individual guest. Molly received a pair of small but powerful binoculars; Em a Chanel lipstick in a limited edition case.

Harry received directions to a cupboard which revealed a leather bound photo album with photos of the café, past and present. Maggie received a beautiful dainty silver salt and pepper pot which entwined around each other, which she adored. Anna passed the final gift to Adam.

She had commissioned one of her favorite local artist to make a keyring of silver in the form of the infinity symbol, which had gems found on the beach worked into the piece, including a tiny glass vile of sand. Anna explained what it represented and contained to Adam. "It's so that you always have a piece of the beach with you when you work away," stated Anna.

Adam hugged her to him. "I love it," he whispered in her ear before he kissed her on the lips, not noticing the surprised glances being exchanged by the other guests.

The group all wrapped up and headed out onto the beach for an afternoon walk. Molly and Em bid their goodbyes as they headed back to Norwich to spend the evening with their dad and grandparents. The rest of the group retired to Maggie's comfortable living room overlooking the sea. Logs cracked in the oversized fireplace and the friends chatted happily.

The private chef had laid out and covered a wonderful buffet in the kitchen for the evening and the drinks flowed. The usual games were played as the friends laughed and bonded further. Maggie stood up. "I would like to propose a toast," she stated as everyone raised their glasses.

"May this get together of family and friends become a festive tradition." As tears welled in her eye's she stated, "I have had such a wonderful day, thank you all for being part of it." She raised her glass to toast, "Merry Christmas."

They all clinked glasses and wished each other Merry Christmas. Every guest had felt the warmth and love the group had built and every eye had the shiny glint of happy emotions. They had no doubt that such a festive and joyous Christmas Day would be repeated.

Chapter 8
And so for a New Year

Christmas day had been a resounding success. It was like being at home with all the security and comfort that gives, but with the hired chef and waiter team, it was like going out for a meal and nobody had the pressure of cooking the meal. Anna smiled as she was closing the cafe on the first Wednesday of the new year, remembering the wonderful day they all had.

Over the last week, she had thought long about her reasoning for not wanting a man in her life. She still wasn't sure she did, but more than anything, she knew it wasn't a man that she didn't want, it was the husband she had that she didn't want in her life. Thankfully, she had left him behind. As Anna continued to finish up the clean down, she suddenly felt the urge to look up.

There, watching her from the beach was said husband. She quickly looked away and continued on, hoping she had imagined it or that he walked on by, either way at that moment, her heart sank. Anna jumped as the café door opened. "Hello, Anna," said Mark. She turned and felt the blood rush out of her and all the old feeling flood back.

Stay composed she told herself, he has no hold on you. "Just thought I would pop by and see how my lovely wife was doing."

"I'm not your wife anymore and I'm fine, just closing up," she stated matter-o-factly.

"Nice little café."

"Thank you, but if you don't mind I want to close up," she stated and ushered towards the door. She did not have to take anything from him anymore, she was free. She had been stuck with him too long, bowed to his views and ways for too long. She felt herself getting angry, how dare he come here!

"So you decided to go after my pension, did you!" This was not a confrontation Anna wanted. Yes, she had applied for a pension sharing order, but he had only contributed since they were together and she was never able to afford to pay into her own pension. While his employment forced the large contributions he made each month direct from his salary into his, so he had built his large pension up while she had not been able to.

Anna felt panicked. "I want you to leave," she stated.

"Don't I even get a cup of tea?"

"I want you to leave please," Anna asked again. "Or I will call the police."

"I am the police," laughed Mark. "What are you going to say, I threatened you with a hello!" Just at that moment, Maggie and Adam walked into the café, much to Anna's relief.

"Hi, Anna, ready for the walk, or are you entertaining," asked Maggie. Maggie of course knew exactly what was going on. She had noticed the man on the beach on several occasion loitering about and she had seen him watching the café. With a little bit of digging, she found out who he was and knew no good would come of it.

On that particular afternoon, he wasn't sleazily sauntering but striding towards the café at speed, Maggie immediately called Adam and they headed over. "No, Mark was just leaving," said Anna as she looked away and continued to finish up cleaning down the café with a huge feeling of relief, but she did notice Adam open the door to the café and usher Mark in that direction, with a look of menace only meant for Mark.

With Maggie and Adam present, Mark had no option but comply, but she saw the rage in his eyes.

During the event, Adam's shoulders seemed to of grown and he looked ready to pounce. Anna felt protected by Adam in a way she had never felt with Mark. He was always looking to trip her up in some way or announce I told you so, not protect her. Adam was the complete opposite.

He didn't ask for anything, he just protected, as he did with Maggie. Maybe his loss had made him hold close those he loved and held dear, to protect them, to make sure that nothing bad happened to them. Anna was so grateful for her new friends; they didn't ask for anything but Anna gave back without even realizing, more than she knew.

Anna was quite shaken by the event and after seeing Mark off. Adam moved to Anna and gave her a hug. Maggie looked on with a caring smile, happy with how her protégées were bonding and how well Anna had settled in. "Right," said Maggie. "You can stay with me for tonight while we talk through how to make sure that such an event like this does not happen again. Adam, you are staying too, just as a precaution?"

Both Anna and Adam opened their mouths to protest, but soon shut them again as Maggie waltzed towards the café door. "Come along," said Maggie as she held the door open. Anna quickly finished locking down the café and the 3 of them headed towards home. All 3 kept their eyes open for Mark.

Adam dropped Anna at her cottage and told her to lock her door. "I'll see Maggie home and will be back for you in an hour." Anna rolled her eyes but knew protesting was pointless. Anna packed an overnight bag, slightly annoyed that her ex-husband had caused her not to be able to stay in her own cottage, but at the same time, she had been unnerved by his arrival so an evening with friends wouldn't be a bad thing.

Adam collected Anna in the truck and headed to Maggie's. Anna did feel that everyone had overreacted, but then she didn't know that Mark had been watching her for a while. Adam wasn't too sure what to think, but he was happy to go with the flow. An evening with his two favorite ladies was just a bonus so he settled in for the evening, enjoying the company and the crackle and warmth of the logs in the fireplace.

A Chinese take-away was ordered. Maggie had administered stiff gin and tonics. Anna recalled what had happened and what Mark had said to her. She stated that he was probably just angry and didn't think it should be anything to worry about, which Adam agreed with. "He probably just needs time to cool down and find his own path."

Maggie nodded. "Ok then, may I suggest that you call the very reasonable ex-husband of yours and ask that he does not visit you again uninvited, and suggest that you will inform his employers if he does. I would like you to add that he has unbeknown to you, been hanging around and watching you for some weeks which is unhealthy."

"What," said Anna.

"Why do you think we arrived when we did. I had noticed him hanging around and didn't like what I saw this afternoon, hence I called Adam and we headed over."

Anna burst out laughing. "You are the Miss Marple of the Norfolk coast!" Adam also laughed at this, as did Maggie. *Miss Marple,* she thought, *ridiculous but it did tickle her sense of humor.*

Chinese eaten and conversations between friends went on into the evening. As it grew late, Maggie stated she was going to retire, both her guests had a bedroom each. Adam's being closest to the entry and exit points, so he was on guard. Not that Anna or Adam thought it was needed at all, but they went along with Maggie's kindness.

Adam knew every inch of Maggie's cottage as he had built it. It was meant to withstand storms, the cottage being of a steel frame construction, pinned into concrete pylons, drilled into the sand. Maggie smiled as she climbed into bed, safe in the knowledge that Adam was looking after them both and fell asleep, tired by the days goings on.

Downstairs, Teddy wanted out to do his last business, Anna and Adam stood on the deck, Anna ready with a poop bag, avidly watching Teddy to make sure she kept the beach clean. Adam headed in to get them a G&T top up and a couple of blankets, so they could watch the moon on the waves. Teddy did his normal circling and Anna strode towards the spot with bag in hand.

As she leant down, she felt a slam on the back of her neck and her face hit the sand, disorientated. She heard Teddy barking and felt a painful wrench as she was dragged along the sand by her hair. Anna was already struggling for breath when she felt the first wave go over her face, then she felt the wave lift her body as she was pulled deeper into the crashing power of the waves.

The cold hit her; she felt her head hit something hard, at that point she lost consciousness. The sound of braking glass on the deck woke Maggie. She stumbled to the window in her sleepy state to see what looked like 2 figures in the moonlit surf, 1 stood, 1 lying face down. She then saw Adam running towards the 2 figures; Maggie turned and picked up her bedroom phone and dialed 999.

Adam had dropped the glasses of G&T on the deck as he realized what was happening and ran towards the 2 figures. He reached the shoreline and punched Mark as hard as he could to make sure he wouldn't prevent him from getting Anna out of the water. Once Anna was safely on shore, he dragged Mark out too and dumped him on the sand away from the sea edge.

Adam checked Anna was still breathing and picked her up, she was like a rag doll in his arms. He saw Maggie as he approached the cottage. "I've called an ambulance and the police," she stated. Adam quickly mounted the stairs and took Anna into the lounge, gently laying her on the couch. Adam spoke to her softly, unsure if she could hear but wanted to reassure her.

He told her she was safe now and that an ambulance was on the way. Maggie had locked the door after Adam but kept an eye on the body on the beach. She wasn't sure what this mad man was capable of and she wasn't taking any chances.

The sound of sirens could be heard, which became louder as they drew closer. Maggie crossed the cottage to let them in. The paramedics arrived first, Maggie showed them to were Anna was laid. The paramedic knelt down next to Anna as Adam relayed to them what he had seen, which wasn't an awful lot.

He explained that he had gone to fetch a drink and returned to the deck to find Anna in the waves being held down by her ex-husband. He wasn't sure how she had got there but could see she had cuts to her face. Adam let the paramedics do their job, as he headed to the beach. Maggie went after him. She knew Adam would have a rage inside him right now.

Thankfully, the police arrived just at that moment and one of them joined Maggie and Adam onto the beach. Much to everyone's surprise, Mark was nowhere to be seen and as the tide was going out, Adam was certain he was not in the water. Maggie and Adam headed back to the cottage as the officers searched for Mark. Maggie had given the officer his full name and that he himself was a police officer.

As they entered Maggie's, they both heaved a sigh of relief as they saw that Anna had regained consciousness and was sat up. The medic had cleaned up the scratches and cuts on her face and applied some dressings to the larger one. The medic had stated he would prefer she went to the hospital but Anna was resisting, insisting she was fine.

The medic addressed both Adam and Anna to check that someone would be with her and to call them if she showed any signs of dizziness, vomiting or anything out of the ordinary. They both agreed. The paramedics suggested she see her GP when she felt ready, for a check-up and bid their goodbyes. Maggie saw them out.

The police officers arrived back from the beach and shook their heads, no-one mentioned a word about Mark. One officer sat down beside Anna and asked if she was feeling well enough to give a statement. Anna agreed and they all sat down to listen as no-one in the room apart from Anna actually knew what had happened.

As Anna revealed that as she was going to clean up after Teddy, her dog, on the beach and that as she leant down she felt a slam on the back of her head and that her face had hit the sand, disorientated. She heard Teddy barking and a painful wrench as she was being dragged along the sand by her hair.

Anna explained that she had struggled for breath when she felt the first wave go over her face. She felt a blow to her head, then she felt the wave lift her body as she was pulled deeper into the surf. She said that she couldn't remember anything after that. The officer asked if Anna knew who had attacked her.

Anna replied, "Yes, it was my ex-husband, Mark, I didn't see him but I knew it was him. The sounds of rage he made and the smell and build, I have no doubt," said Anna. The officer thanked Anna and looked at Adam and Maggie. Adam had stood up and started to pace the room as Anna had recounted the events.

Adam gave his account of what had happened and that he could confirm it was Mark. It was at this point that Anna gasped at hearing that Mark had disappeared. Adam felt a pang of guilt and a surge of anger at this point. *He should have hit him harder,* he thought.

He also gave an accord of what had happened in the café earlier, and Maggie and Anna backed this up. Anna giving the extra details about what Mark had said about the pension sharing order she had applied for and what Mark had said in the café. The officer explained that a warrant had been issued for Mark's arrest and asked what Anna's plans were for the next few days.

Adam had then interjected that Anna would not be let out of his sight until Mark had been arrested. Anna went to protest, but then thought better of it, she would feel safer with Adam. The officer stated that they should dial 999 if they had any further visits form Mark and that an officer would be over tomorrow to do a welfare check and give them an update on Mark's location.

As the officers left, Maggie arrived with a tray of stiff G&T's. "Well," stated Maggie, "that was eventful," as she took a large gulp of drink, both Anna and Adam burst out laughing. The three of them discussed sleeping arrangements and Adam had smiled as Maggie suggested that he should sleep in with Anna, then that he would sleep outside her door.

Then finally it was agreed that the two girls would take their own rooms but leave the doors open, and Adam would sleep in his room with his door open too. He was happy that the building was locked tight and secure as he had fitted the house out with security in mind, knowing that Maggie would be living there alone.

The rest of the night was thankfully uneventful. The next morning, the three of them discussed a plan of action over breakfast. "I need to open the café," stated Anna.

"We are not sure if you received concussion as yet, Anna. I think it best you take the rest of the week off," stated Maggie.

Thankfully, Anna agreed and Maggie called Harry to put a note on the door and briefly explained what had happened so he could keep his wits about him also.

"I think for the next couple of days we should all stay at my place, you included, Maggie," said Adam. "Mark knows who you are and this place now. For both of your safety, it may be wise until Mark is picked up. We don't know or understand what Mark's mental state is at the moment."

"Oh my goodness," stated Anna as she stood up and startled the other two. "The girls," stated Anna. "Are they safe and what do I tell them?" Anna put her hands to her face and sat back down. No one knew the answer to that.

"Maybe this is something we could ask the officer when he calls today," stated Adam. "In the meantime, do I have agreement on staying at my place?" All agreed reluctantly.

Maggie packed a bag and Adam called the local police station to let them know where they would be. He also called a friend who was a local cabbie to collect them, drive them to Anna's to collect her bag then onto Adam's. By mid-afternoon, they were all settled at Adam's.

When the police officer called, there had been no sightings of Mark and he had not shown up for work. They had visited his home and there was no sign of him. Anna spoke to the officer about the girls and he advised they were told. He did not feel they would be in any danger but felt they should know.

There were calls that Anna was not looking forward to make, but make she must. Anna still felt quite shaken from the previous night's events and after encouragement, went for a soak in the bath. Thankfully, Adam's beach house had 3 bedrooms and all had en-suite bathrooms. Adam and Maggie sat in Adam's upstairs living room looking out to sea.

They both spoke softly. "That animal tried to kill Anna," exclaimed Maggie. "The police should be doing everything they possibly can to find him."

"I'm sure they are," stated Adam. "But yes, in his state of mind, he is very dangerous. So as long as he is at large, we need to keep him from Anna."

After her bath, Anna made the calls to her daughters. Both were shocked but Anna had downplayed it, saying he had lashed out at her in anger and telling them she didn't think their father was quite himself at the moment. She encouraged the girls to call their nana, so she was aware if not already.

Mark's mother lived close to both the them and Anna knew she would look after the girls. She also knew that if anyone could talk Mark down, it was her. Anna also told the girls to call the police if they had any concerns and that she felt it would not be wise to visit until their father was found. The girls reluctantly agreed.

That evening the 3 friends settled in at Adam's. He rustled up a pasta meal and had selected a nice bottle of wine to go with it. Adam had an impressive wine cellar. He served up a wonderful chilled Chablis which complimented it perfectly. The 3 friends cleared up and settled in front of the fire.

Adam had shut all curtains just before night fell and before any lights were turned on to make sure no-one could see in. He knew his house was secure as he had added extra security. As he worked away and wanted to make sure that while he was away, no-one could get in and raid his wine cellar or any of the precious items he had collected over the years and he now had inside.

Both Maggie and Adam had let their close and trusted friends know what had happened and where they were all staying, partly so they were aware but also to ask they keep an eye out for Mark. He had also asked that when out and about or close by, that they take a detour past Adam's house in case Mark was lurking.

Maggie retired early, exhausted by the events of the last couple of days. Anna and Adam relaxed and chatted while watching the logs flicker in Adam's fireplace which fascinated Anna. "It's like a UFO which has come down from the ceiling."

Adam laughed. "It's meant to be contemporary but to be honest, I just loved the shape of it."

That evening, Adam avoided all conversation about the previous night events, as he thought Anna hadn't realized the enormity of what Mark had attempted and Adam didn't want Anna to think about it. "Thank you, Adam, for always being there for me."

Adam smiled. "I love your crazy life," he laughed.

"It's not normally this crazy."

"How's the head?" He asked as he looked at the dressing on her forehead.

"I think I need to get the dressings changed, cleaned or removed. I dare not look to be honest."

"Give me a moment," stated Adam and he disappeared, arriving back with and impressive first aid kit.

"I didn't realize you practiced medicine as well," teased Anna.

"When you work on building sites, you never know what you might have to deal with and I've had my fair share of dealings, so I try to keep a kit which enables me to treat or patch to prevent further damage, before the professionals arrive." Adam walked to the kitchen and washed his hands before turning on the overhead light and taking a look at Anna's dressings.

The superficial scratches were healing nicely, but the dressings did need changing. Adam dabbed at the stuck on dressings with saline and cotton wool to ease their release. Anna should have really had a nurse to do this but right now he didn't think Mark knew where Anna was, so he was happy to act as nurse this evening. The main cuts and grazes covered just one side of her face.

She had a nasty gash on the side of her forehead and another large one on her cheek, with 3 other smaller cuts running from her forehead down her cheek. "They all look quite good," said Adam. The larger cuts had sterry stitches applied to help them heal quicker. Adam left these in place but gave them all a good clean by gently patting them with antiseptic wipes.

Anna liked the feeling of having Adam close. He had been so kind, gentle and protective of her, she almost wished this bubble would never burst. He had large strong hands but was so careful with her injuries. He wore a subtle but manly scent which has a sweetness to it, like a musky jasmine. He had a strong, lean body which Anna couldn't help but notice.

He re-dressed the gash on her forehead and the 3 on her cheek. "Better?" He asked.

"Yes," said Anna as she looked up into his eyes. He kissed her gently on the lips, and sat back down. Anna again thought that she hadn't wanted a man in her life, but this man, she liked being around. Adam wanted to take Anna in his arms but knew it was too soon, especially after what had just happened. They chatted and laughed for another hour or so before they both retired to bed. Adam left his door open.

Chapter 9

Mark was enraged. When he picked himself up off the beach, he heard the sirens and headed for his car. He booked into a local hotel and plotted how to destroy Anna and her perfect little set up. He had missed calls from his mother and daughters but all he could think about was destroying Anna.

He was her husband and she was his wife, and he had no intention of letting any further developments happen in her happy little life. He had been to the café and Maggie's house, he had scoured the beach and taken a room at a different local hotel closer to Anna's cottage where he could prop up the bar and wait till someone gave an inkling of where Anna may be.

As the days ticked by, he kept himself to himself and avoided any sight of the police. He had turned off his phone and made sure he tipped the staff well. He was willing to wait.

Anna felt better for having her injuries re-dressed the night before and woke up feeling safe and happy. The next morning, the 3 of them ate breakfast of pasties freshly delivered that morning at 8am. Adam had ordered a grocery delivery and took advantage of a good fresh breakfast selection of pasties, along with a ham, a free range chicken and a few other joints, lots of salad and vegetables amongst many other things, so they could cook and eat in until Mark was found.

Maggie joked as they unpacked the shopping, that maybe a great storm was coming and Adam would start allowing animals in two by two. It was a strangely happy time, a little like Christmas when time stands still. Maggie was like a mother hen, forever making cups of tea and observing the goings on of the beach walkers, reporting back like a look-out.

Anna felt happier and to a certain extent healed, both emotionally and physically, as the 3 friends moved to the lounge in their strange bubble. All 3 knew this chat was coming.

"So," said Anna, Adam and Maggie were expecting this, "we can't stay cooped up like this forever," stated Anna. There was a long pause as neither Adam or Maggie knew how to broach the subject. Adam cleared his throat.

"Anna," Adam paused, "Mark tried to kill you and if we had not been there, I have no doubt that he would have achieved it. He is still out there and we don't know his emotional state or intentions, but I believe that if he is not caught he will try it again. The actions he has taken will mean that he will lose his job and possibly his freedom, which means he has nothing to lose and that makes him very dangerous," stated Adam.

He paused before he said that he would call the station to see if there is any news as he headed downstairs to find his phone. Maggie had a long talk with Anna who agreed for now to stay put. Having lost both her parents, there was something comforting about being in this bubble. She also knew that Adam was right and that Maggie would be at risk if she went home, especially at the moment, which was something she couldn't chance.

Adam called the local police station for an update. No news, which concerned Adam. While he was still at large, he was a threat to everyone he held dear and it frustrated Adam that he couldn't do anything about it, but he knew the best place for him was right where he was. Adam strode back upstairs and got the nod from Maggie.

"Right, ladies, let's do a joint effort Sunday Roast."

"But it's not Sunday," stated Anna.

"I declare that in our bubble, it is Sunday," stated Adam. "After dinner, we can close up for a movie night and popcorn!" Maggie jumped to her feet in excitement clapping her hands like a school girl.

All 3 of them happily prepared the roast. Adam had purchased several joints and a chicken in his grocery order and intended to cook the beef rib joint which was now in and the vegetables were being prepared. "Do any of you like cauliflower cheese?" Anna asked.

Adam started with "Do bears…" hushed by Maggie.

"An absolute favorite of mine," stated Maggie.

"Fabulous," stated Anna. "I was the only one in my family that liked it, that's my job then." Adam looked after the beef, red cabbage (another favorite they all discovered they liked) along with laying the table. Anna did the cauliflower cheese and Yorkshire puddings and Maggie looked after the veg and potatoes. Once all was prepped and on its way cooking, Adam announced pre-dinner drinks.

Naturally, they had to sit back from the windows, but close enough to enjoy watching the waves. It really was like a private haven. The 3 friends chatted happily with the smell of the roast becoming more delicious as elements came closer to being cooked, enjoying each other's company and the view of the ocean and dog walkers.

All 3 were on lookout naturally but also enjoying the afternoon together. Dinner was delicious. Adam had selected a nice bottle of red to drink and the 3 of them ate dinner at a leisurely pace. After dinner, the three friends chattered as they cleared up.

It was Indeed like a Sunday afternoon back in the 1970s, when the projector would come out to watch old movies and holiday cine films. Adam had a cinema screen that came down from the ceiling. As the screen lowered, Anna stated, "It's a good job you have black out blinds or we would need to start pegging sleeping bags to the curtain polls."

All 3 of them laughed, remembering doing just that. Adam was about to lower the blinds as Maggie and Anna chattered, Anna suddenly stopped speaking mid-sentence and the blood drained out of her face. There on the beach, about 6 meters from the beach house to the left, was Mark watching her intently.

Neither Maggie or Adam could see him from where they were, Anna could only see Mark from the shoulder up. He must have caught sight of them and positioned himself where he could only see and be seen by Anna. "Anna?" Adam asked.

"Mark," was all she could say. Adam jumped in the direction of Anna's gaze, practically launching himself over the upstairs balcony onto the deck below and circling round the house in the direction Anna was looking on the beach below. Maggie by this time was on the phone to the police.

Adam caught sight of Mark running towards the back of the cottage and within a few moments, Adam had caught up with him and launched himself at Mark in a ruby type tackle to take him down. Both men landed on the sand. Adam felt something sharp slice across his shoulder as he grappled with Mark to try and detain him.

He then saw the knife in Mark's right hand and gripped his wrist with his left hand to keep the weapon at arm's reach. Adam managed to pin Mark down long enough on the sand to bring his right fist down to connect with Mark's temple. As he felt a weakening in the other man, Adam started to rain down the punches having prised the knife out of Mark's hand and launch it out of reach.

Adam didn't hear the sirens or the screams from Anna and Maggie to stop, until two dog walkers pulled him off Mark's lifeless body.

Mark was rushed to hospital and Adam was detained by the police. A crowd had gathered outside Adam's beach house as Maggie hurried Anna inside. Dusk was falling and Maggie closed all the curtains and locked all the doors. Anna was sat in the living room looking into space, clearly in shock.

The police had wanted to interview them both but Maggie managed to convince the local sergeant, a friend of hers, to leave it until the morning, reassuring him they would remain where they were. Maggie fetched large G&Ts. "Are you ok, Anna?" As the words came out she thought what a stupid question, but then what else could she say!

Anna took a gulp of the G&T. Maggie gave her a reassuring hug and stated she was popping to the loo where she called the doctor.

Maggie was concerned for Adam but knew he had been there before and how strong he was. They both understood his fiery explosions, he had been pushed to the limit again and snapped. It was understandable and Adam was just trying to protect Maggie and Anna. She just hoped the authorities would see it in the same light.

Anna was still in a daze when the doctor arrived. He was aware of what had happened and was a good friend of Maggie's. Without even realizing it, Anna was put to bed and sedated. Dr Pinto stated that a good night's sleep would be the best thing for now.

Maggie agreed as she thanked him and saw him out, locked up and called Tom, the local sergeant, for an update on Adam. Tom informed Maggie that Adam had been taken to hospital due to a shoulder injury. Maggie wasn't aware of the knife injury Adam had sustained. Because of the severity of Mark's injuries, Adam would have to be held in hospital under police arrest for the night.

Tom reassured Maggie that he would visit in the morning and after discussions, Tom felt that after Anna and Maggie had given statements, Adam would be released. Maggie was happy Adam was being looked after and headed to bed herself, safe in the knowledge that Mark was under lock and key.

Anna awoke disorientated the next morning. She wasn't sure what was real; had yesterday been a dream or a nightmare. She headed upstairs to find some answers. Maggie was up and made Anna a cup of tea. They sat down and Anna opened her mouth but wasn't sure what to say so shut it again and took a sip of tea.

"How are you feeling, my dear?" Maggie asked.

"Confused," said Anna. "Did I dream yesterday? Please say Adam is in bed having a lay in," hoping it was just a weird dream.

"I'm afraid not," stated Maggie. "But he is ok and in good hands. The good news is that Mark is under lock and key. I have a feeling he may remain there for some time to come," stated Maggie. Anna sat for a few moments, then asked Maggie what exactly had happened as she felt like it was all a blur.

Maggie explained every moment from start to finish including Anna's shock and the sedative the doctor had given her, which gave Anna relief as she had thought she was going slightly mad. "Where is Adam now," asked Anna.

"Under hospital arrest, but Tom, the local sergeant, a close friend of mine, has promised me he will be well looked after, and he believes he will be released without charge once we give our statements." Anna asked which hospital Adam was in. Maggie was unsure, but stood to phone Tom. Anna headed for a shower.

Maggie had spoken with Tom and he wanted to take the statements from both of them. Maggie had asked if he could come over straight away as she knew Anna would be wanting to see Adam. A couple of police officers arrived just as Anna was making her way up to the living room. The statements took forever. At least 2 hours which made Anna restless.

She called the girls while Maggie finished her statement. Anna and Maggie had both kept the girls in the loop, down played of course but due to the threat Mark had posed, Anna didn't want the girls with her. Now that Mark had been arrested the girls were keen to come over. Anna arranged for them to come at the weekend.

Maggie and Anna headed over to the hospital to see Adam. There was a policeman sat outside Adam's room. Adam was sleeping as they arrived, propped up in the hospital bed with covers drawn up to his belly button and his top was bare. He had dressings taped to his shoulder and his arm was in a black sling.

Anna couldn't help but notice the definition of Adam's powerful shoulder muscles and sculpted chest, it showed that the work he did was manual and took strength. Maggie caught sight of Anna and smiled. Anna reddened and looked for chairs for them both. Maggie went to get coffees and to call Tom to see if their statements had secured Adam's release from police custody.

Anna sat beside Adam and reached for his hand, at which point Adam opened his eyes. "How are you feeling?" Anna asked, stupid question but it broke the air.

"I've been better but I'm fine. How are you?" He asked.

"I'm fine," replied Anna.

Adam gingerly moved himself to sit up. "I just want to get out of here, is my friend still at the door," asked Adam.

"Yes, for now," stated Anna. "Maggie and I both gave statements this morning which we are told should secure your release." Adam squeezed her hand and smiled. "I would have been here earlier but they took forever!" Anna stated. "Did you hear about Mark?"

"Yes," stated Adam. "At least, you are safe now and you can start to get back to normal," said Adam. Anna wondered why this made Anna feel sad. At that moment, they both looked towards the door as they could hear Maggie directing proceedings outside. A few minutes later, Maggie appeared followed by the police officer.

"I'll be off now," stated the officer. "You are free to go once the doc has ok'd it. Take care of yourself, Adam," smiled the officer.

"Thanks, Jake," said Adam as he smiled towards the officer, and lifted the un-injured arm to shake the officer's hand.

Once the officer had left, Adam immediately swung his legs to the floor. "What are you doing, Adam?" Maggie asked.

"I have no intention of staying here any longer than I need to, ladies," he motioned to the door as he stood before them in his boxer shorts. Maggie and Anna both headed for the door. Maggie headed to the ward reception to get a low down on Adam's care going forward and to inform them he was discharging himself.

Anna lingered at the door. She figured that Adam would need some help with his shirt. After a few minutes, she heard Adam curse so knocked on the door. "Come in," stated Adam. Anna walked in to find Adam with one arm in the t-shirt they had brought along with another few items, figuring the clothes he had arrived in would be in a bit of a mess.

Adam sat on the bed looking perplexed. Anna smiled and walked towards him. "My turn to help you." She smiled as she carefully took the t-shirt off his good arm and carefully passed the sleeve over his bad arm and sling, then over his head and good arm, dressing him as she would a child with care and love.

"Smart-arse," smiled Adam, which made Anna laugh.

"I've felt pretty useless over the last few days, so it's good to be of use at last."

Maggie arrived in the room with a hospital wheel chair, took one look at Adam and wheeled the chair straight back out. Anna laughed, she had a feeling Adam was going to be a stubborn patient. At that moment, she decided she would stay on at Adam's for a few days more till he was more mobile.

No matter how hard Adam protested, at least that was the excuse she gave herself, not wanting to admit that she enjoyed being with Adam.

She would set a date for re-opening the café and post it on the door. She knew all her regulars would know what had gone on and would understand.

They arrived back at Adam's late afternoon. Anna had told Maggie that she was going to stay on and look after Adam for a few days. Unbeknown to Anna, Maggie was delighted, but didn't show it. "Good idea, my dear," stated Maggie, smiling at how the course of events had brought Adam and Anna even closer.

Maggie considered the two of them as family and lost souls, who she believed would make the perfect couple and so, from the moment she got to know Anna, Maggie had hatched a plan to bring them together. Not quite expecting the course of events which had played out over the last few days, but all the same it seemed to cement their bond and that pleased Maggie. They both deserved to be happy and she believed they would make each other that way.

Adam had sustained a cut to his trapezius muscle which supports the movement to the arm. It was still attached thankfully but it was vital he kept his injured arm as stable as possible to avoid further damage and to allow it to heal as quickly as possible.

Maggie bid her goodbyes once Adam was settled. Adam thanked her for everything. Maggie kissed him on the forehead and smiled as she told him to be a good patient, before she headed out the door. Adam looked slightly confused since he was out of hospital. "I am going to stay on for a few days until you are more mobile," stated Anna expecting a protest from Adam.

To her surprise, he smiled. "I think this calls for a celebration!" Anna asked why. "You and Maggie are safe and well; I'm alive and not in a police station; Mark is behind bars and I have a nurse to die for!"

Anna laughed. "You well could have," exclaimed Anna.

"As could have you, Anna." stated Adam. Anna thought for a moment about the events of the past few days then stood quickly.

"I totally agree," said Anna. "We should celebrate." and she headed towards the fridge. "What do you have in mind?" Anna asked as she opened the fridge and a bottle of Taittinger stared her in the face.

"The glasses are on the top."

"I know," said Anna with a smile. Anna lit a fire and sat on the sofa with her legs crossed opposite Adam as she sipped her favorite champagne. *Progress,* thought Adam.

The two sat and chatted about nothing in particular, sipping on their glorious bubbles. "How are you feeling?" Anna asked.

"Sore and in need of a shower, but I'm not going anywhere till we've finished this champagne."

Anna smiled. "Agreed, then I will help you to shower and dress, then I will try and rustle something up for tea."

"That sounds perfect," stated Adam. Anna headed to the fridge and took out the bottle of champagne and poured them both another glass; they clinked glasses in a toast. The fire was crackling, the curtains were open and the waves rolled.

Anna and Adam both thought that the afternoon couldn't be better. Anna stretched out her foot and rested it on Adams.

Another hour passed and the two friends became even more comfortable in each other's company. They spoke about everything and anything. Anna regularly topped up the fire with wood neatly stacked beside the levitating bulbous fireplace. "Right," said Anna. "Shower time!"

Adam groaned but agreed, Anna helped him up and followed him to his bedroom, It was simple and clean. It had a solid dark wooden bed which looked king-size, with crisp white pillows and a quilt which looked very puffy. Anna was quite tired and could have easily just sunk into it.

There were dark wood dressers and a large upholstered wooden chair in the corner which could easily fit 3. At the end of the bed was a large upholstered ottoman, in the same muted colors as the chair and there were two bedside tables with lamps either side of the bed with blown glass jar style bases and muted shades with a cooper sheen to the inside of the shade.

Anna took it all in as Adam tried to undress. Anna turned and couldn't help but laugh at Adam unsuccessfully trying to remove his t-shirt. "Sorry, I'm meant to be helping." Both of them were slightly merry with the champagne. Anna helped Adam remove his t-shirt and went to start the shower.

After a bit of trial and error, she returned slightly wet, but a warm shower was running. Adam needed to keep his arm stabilized but needed to take off the sling. Adam stood as Anna undid his trousers. She looked up at him with a wry smile and he rolled his eyes and then he sat on the bed as she removed them.

"Right sling or boxer shorts, which first?" Anna asked.

"Wow, you really know how to romance a fellah." They were both already having trouble containing their laughter at the whole situation. Adam moved his good arm around Anna's waist and drew her to him. The feeling of Adam's body against her made Anna feel light-headed.

Adam bent down and kissed her, Anna fell into his one handed embrace. As they separated, Anna drew down Adam's boxes and he stepped out of them. She then slowly and carefully removed the sling. Adam one handily started to unbutton Anna's blouse.

Anna undressed without words and Adam led Anna into the shower, with his injured arm still held to his chest. Anna slowly and gently soaped and cleaned Adam's body. She noticed the traces of dried blood left from last night and allowed tears to run down her face as she washed the traces away, allowing the shower to wash her tears away too.

Adam hadn't missed that and drew her to him. They stood together as the warm water washed over them. Anna put both arms around Adams waist and rested her head against his chest and cried. She felt the fingers of Adam's good arm draw her closer as he rested his head on hers, moving his hand to stroke the back of her head.

Anna looked up at him as the water flowed down her face. Adam kissed her forehead, then her lips, then her forehead again and again held her close, letting the water wash away the troubles of the last few days. Anna felt her shoulders ease as the water took away the harshness of what they had encountered and looked up at Adam.

He smiled down at her, seeing the tears had washed away at least some of Anna's pain. "Shall we get out?" Anna asked.

"No, I want to stay here forever," smiled Adam. A few minutes later Anna turned off the shower. "Spoil-sport," laughed Adam.

Anna ticked off Adam as he moved out of the shower too briskly. "If you want your shoulder to heal, you need to keep it in situ." Adam smiled and allowed Anna to dry him off. Anna was slow and methodical. She realized she was helplessly falling in love with him and hoped he felt the same.

Anna couldn't help but notice the strong contours of Adam's body as she dried him off. She could also see that Adam was exhausted, they hadn't eaten tea, but Anna felt sleep may be a better healer right now. She could cook him a hearty breakfast.

Anna laid back the white quilt of the bed and Adam sat down and laid back. "Sorry, I'm not the greatest company tonight," said Adam. Anna got into the king-sized bed on the other side.

"You are the greatest company I could need right now," stated Anna. "And maybe at some point tonight, I will find you in the vastness of this humongous bed." Adam reached over with his good arm and drew her to him and they slept soundly, both feeling a happiness in their closeness.

Anna woke early and breathed in the smell of Adam; a smell she liked, manly but fresh. She carefully moved out of the bed, not wanting to wake him, knowing the sleep would do him good. Anna headed to her bedroom and text Maggie for yet another favor. The house was depleted of groceries and Anna wanted to honor her promise of a cooked breakfast.

Anna showered and headed upstairs, drawing the curtains open and allowing herself a moment to enjoy the sight of the waves. Adam's house was solid and sturdy, but gave views of the amazing outside world, while filling you with the luxuries of the home within. Anna made a cup of tea and heard the ping of a text.

Maggie had already pre-empted the fact that Adam may crash and need a hearty breakfast, so she was already out when she got Anna's text. Maggie was a moment away and didn't want to wake Adam, so Anna popped down to collect the groceries. She weirdly felt sudden panic at opening the door but ignored it. Maggie and Anna chatted on the doorstep, Maggie didn't want to come in.

"Adam needs rest as do you," said Maggie as she waived and drove off. Anna took the package into the house and locked the door. She still wanted to be sure Mark was still locked up, though she felt a sadness for him. They had been married for 20 years and had started off as friends.

It was such a shame it had all come to this. Unfortunately, he seemed to have 20 years of hatred pent up. Anna headed up to cook breakfast, shrugging off any thought of her past life.

Maggie did not disappoint with the delivery for breakfast and Anna set about preparing the table. There was freshly squeezed orange juice, croissants, pastries, eggs, bacon, sausages, mushrooms, melon and berries, natural yogurt, honey, jam and marmalade and fresh bread and butter.

Anna put the bacon and sausages on and put the plates in to warm. She made of platter of the pastries and another of the melon and berries, clinging them to keep them fresh till Adam was up. Anna decanted the butter into two small pots for each of them.

The table was laid as you would expect to see when you go down for breakfast in a posh hotel, with side plates, cutlery, napkins and a jug of milk. She also placed some pain killers close by as she knew Adam would need these once he'd lined his stomach.

Anna heard Adam stir. She had put the sausages and bacon in a dish to hold them warm in the oven while she went downstairs to see if she could help him. Adam was sat on the bed looking frustrated. "How are you feeling?" Anna asked.

"Still sore," stated Adam.

"Do you want a shower?" Anna asked. Adam looked up and smiled. "Ok, let me help you into your dressing gown and we can have breakfast, once that's gone done we can get you showered and dressed," stated Anna. Adam smiled again and Anna rolled her eyes. Anna headed back upstairs to finish up the breakfast, cook the eggs and make a pot of tea.

Adam was impressed by the breakfast spread. "Wow, you have been busy."

"I had a little help from Maggie," stated Anna. Adam smiled and sat down at the table and grabbed a croissant. After he had finished it, Anna handed him the pain killers and stood over him while he washed them down with orange juice. The two of them enjoyed a leisurely breakfast.

They both felt relaxed, glancing at the waves and walkers going by without any impending threat; they chatted and laughed. Anna could see the color come back into Adam's face. She was intent on making sure he healed as soon as possible. Adam ate a good breakfast and for the two of them, time stood still.

Anna told Adam when the girls were arriving and asked if they could stay at Adam's. It made more sense, having everyone together. Adam was more than happy. He loved having the girls around and would like to get to know her daughters better.

Anna cleared up the breakfast, it was now mid-afternoon. They both took a cup of tea to the sofa and sat close to each other watching the waves. "Shall I help you shower and re-dress your shoulder before the girls arrive?" Anna asked. She rolled her eyes at his smile again.

There was no reason for Anna to join Adam in the shower, but she did anyway and gently washed him down, giving him a stern look whenever he moved his shoulder. Adam raised his chin and let the water run over his face. He let out a deep sigh as he looked down at Anna. She could see what was on Adam's mind but now was not the time.

Anna dried Adam off and helped him dress in comfortable jeans and a t-shirt. She had cleaned and re-dressed his shoulder wound; the stitches were tidy and the wound was knitting together already. Adam sat in the large armchair while Anna cleared up his bedroom.

As they chattered, Adam stood once she was finished and kissed her on the forehead. "Thank you, Anna," he smiled.

"I should be thanking you," she replied. Adam used his good arm to stroke away the strand of hair which fell down across her forehead and leant down to kiss her on the lips. They both savored the moment and Anna put her arms around his waist.

The two of them had bonded though this strange experience. They were both scared of getting close to another person again, but it seemed like it may be out of their control.

Chapter 10
And so Life Changes

Adam was asleep on the sofa when Anna arrived upstairs. She had tidied up and changed Adam's blood stained sheets and had made up clean beds for the girls. Anna busied herself in preparation of her daughters arrival. Teddy had been in hiding at Harry's and the girls were going to collect him on their way.

The three of them arrived at Adam's. Teddy was first up the stairs and he couldn't help his excitement. Molly was next; she bounded into Adam's place and hurtled up the stairs. "Wow, this place is amazing," she said as she headed out onto the upstairs balcony and immediately saw something which set her into a fit of giggles.

"She's contagious," laughed Adam as he stood and walked over to see what Molly found so funny. The two of then laughed and giggled, as they leant over the balcony. Partly at the antics of the beach walkers and partly at Molly's creative view of the antics and the commentary she added. Anna smiled, she had a feeling they would get on.

Both girls had met Adam on Christmas day, but that was purely platonic. things had now slightly changed and with what had happened with their father. Anna wasn't entirely sure how to address it.

For now, Molly was happy and laughing. Anna couldn't really ask for more. Em was settling into her room. Once everyone was gathered, Anna helped Adam to pour everyone a drink and they all sat on the sofa musing over what to order from the Chinese. A happy evening was had.

They did discuss the girl's father. Obviously they were both upset about it and felt sad that their father would be spending some time behind bars, due to what he had done. Neither girls could understand what had come over their father. They had known he was a control freak who couldn't take no for an answer, but both were truly shocked by his actions.

Both girls had spoken to their father over the phone but neither had discussed why or what had happened. They had kept it platonic, partly because none had known what to say. They had sent each other their love and told their dad to look after himself, unsure of how a policeman would be treated in prison.

The following morning, they all walked along the beach. Naturally, stopping off at Maggie's who hugged them all and served tea and pastries. They chatted and laughed in Maggie's cozy cottage, avoiding discussion of the violent events which involved their father. They had planned to go to Adam's favorite restaurant 'Rocky Bottom', just outside Cromer for dinner and invited Maggie along.

It would be good to get dressed up and go out. The restaurant served delicious seafood and has amazing views over the Norfolk coastline. Adam was good friends with the restaurant owner and had reserved a table upstairs. As it was low season, he had agreed they could have the upstairs to themselves.

Local press and residents were starting to get to know snippets of what had happened and Adam wanted to protect all involved. He also knew that it was only a matter of time before the press got and published details. He was afraid what intrusion and effect this would have on Anna, Maggie and the girls.

Everyone enjoyed getting ready for a night out and the normality it brought. Anna and Adam both had a G&T and settled in the lounge ready for the taxi to arrive. Molly had dressed down. She looked stunning as usual, with her long wavy hair, she had her own sense of style regardless of what she wore. She always looked like a rock chic, with her rolling stones T-shirt and oversized denim shirt, jeans and pumps.

Maggie had organized a 7-seater with the local taxi firm. Maggie naturally knew the owner and the owner knew what had gone on, so he sent his most trusted driver and instructed he wait outside the restaurant till they were ready to leave. Adam had organized for the driver to have a meal delivered to him so he was well fed while he waited.

All the staff were briefed on the sensitivity of the situation so that if the press did get to know the story, they would be prepared to keep their guests protected.

The taxi picked up Maggie first, then Anna, Adam and the girls. Thankfully, the drive over was uneventful and they settled at their table, happy and looking forward to the meal. A few of the local guests did stare at the group and they could all see the whispers and interest in them.

Thankfully, Adam had realized this might be the case and they were easily ushered upstairs to their awaiting table. "I feel like a celeb," laughed Molly. Em rolled her eyes. Anna smiled at her daughter and gave her a hug. Maggie and Adam looked at each other and realized it was only a matter of time before the full story broke; unsure how they were going to protect Anna and the girls from the potential media interest.

The girls had not been told exactly what happened and they hadn't asked. Adam and Maggie were both afraid if the press got involved. The full details may come out and they were both fearful of the impact this could have on the girls. Especially, if the press start offering financial gain to any locals who may have seen elements of the events.

Adam dreaded how the story could be exaggerated, even depicted as it actually happened would have a massive impact on the girls, both Adam and Maggie were concerned, they both hoped they could fly under the radar without any press picking it up.

The meal did not disappoint, everyone decided on the seafood platter with fresh bread. Lobster, crab, oysters, prawns, brown shrimp, mussels and clams. The meal was an event, everyone in the party loved shellfish and all took time enjoying their meal, with finger bowls to clean their hands and plenty of napkins.

Adam ordered Chablis and spring water, along with the odd cocktail which Molly suggested. All picked over the shellfish, chatting and laughing. It was a relief of normality for all of them. After dinner, coffee was ordered and some partook in the delicious deserts on offer with local ice-cream.

As they enjoyed their coffee, the owner motioned to Adam to come over. He excused himself without causing concern, but he had a sinking feeling that the news was not good.

Jake, the owner, was informed of what had gone on and held Adam in high regard as a close friend. Adam had also been fundamental in the building of his restaurant and had helped Jake out when finances when they were tight. Jake had been monitoring the news and it was not looking good.

The headlines read 'Police Officers attempts to murder ex-wife and lover on the Norfolk coast'. Adam swore; this was exactly what he had been afraid of. There were also press in the car park. Adam was surprised that they knew they were there, but there was a chance a local who saw them arrive could have put something out.

Adam informed his party of what was happening and Jake helped Adam get everyone out of the restaurant and home via a trip in the back of his refrigerated van. Molly thought this very 007. The rest of the party were not so enthusiastic but understood and it succeeded. The press stayed where they were for now, unaware that their pray had already driven away, if they knew they were there at all.

Adam knew the press would know their locations by the morning if not before. They agreed the girls should head home that evening and Adam called Em's partner, who agreed to collect them. Molly was reluctant to go, but Anna convinced her knowing the focus would be on her and Adam, once more details came out.

Anna had already closed all of her social media and suggested her daughters did the same, in the hope that the media couldn't link and find them. Anna kissed and hugged her daughters goodbye, deeply saddened by the fact that the interest in what had gone on meant her separation from her daughters. She was unsure if they would be safe from the media, but knew she wanted to try her best to protect them.

Maggie was insistent she would sit it out. She would not be the main focus of attention, though she secretly liked the thought of it. Adam and Anna smiled and hugged Maggie goodbye, thinking similar thoughts regarding the media attention Maggie might get.

Once the girls had been collected, Adam instructed Anna to pack a bag with what she had. "Anything you don't have, we can buy." It was late evening as they both got into Adam's cab with Teddy and hit the road. The plan was to get some distance between them and find a hotel for the night, then rent a remote cottage somewhere.

They hoped that if the press couldn't find them they would lose interest in the story. Anna drove while Adam was tasked with finding a hotel on route. They booked into a Doubletree by Dartford Tunnel and arrived in the early hours. They shared a room and bed, both exhausted, they both slept soundly.

Anna woke and opened her eyes to find Adam on his laptop. He was sat on the bed just in his boxer shorts, with his legs outstretched and the laptop open on the bed between his legs. Anna watched him for a while before Adam sensed her gaze and looked back at her. "Morning," he smiled.

"Good morning," replied Anna, wondering what tricks fate had planned for them.

"I took the liberty to have breakfast delivered to our room," stated Adam as he motioned towards the TV, where a photo of Anna and her ex-husband had just popped up with the headlines, 'Respected Police Officer in custody, charged with attempting to murder his ex-wife and her partner'. A photo of Adam was shown next as Adam switched off the TV.

"Wow," said Anna, "that didn't take long!"

"I suspected as much," stated Adam, matter-a-factly.

When room service arrived, Anna ducked into the bathroom and Adam made sure he kept his face from view just in case. They ate breakfast leisurely. It was a bit of a forced but exciting adventure and Adam was keen for Anna to feel like this too. He felt it himself and he had to admit, he rather liked it. Life was far too planned and contrived and right now, that was very far from the truth.

They both mused over cottages to rent. As it was low season, there was a good choice. It was bit like a couple planning a holiday. The one thing they both agreed on was a sea view and it needed to be remote. They came across a beautiful old beach hut, once home to a sea captain and passed down through the generations.

Now brought up to date with floor to ceiling windows, perched on a cliff in Whitsand Bay, Cornwall. Complete with wood-burner and hot-tub on the deck overlooking the sea. "One double bedroom?" Adam stated, almost as a question.

"I can live with that if you can," stated Anna. Adam smiled at Anna and Anna rolled her eyes smiling too. "That's sorted then," as he booked the property for the next 3 weeks. Unsure how long they would need to stay, but hoped the news might die down by then, if not before.

The journey would take a little over 4 hours. Anna booked a click and collect at a grocery store near their destination, calling out suggestion and discussing with Adam what they might need. They wanted to keep their need to go out to a minimum, so they planned meals and shopped accordingly. Anna enjoyed being with Adam and discovering his likes from the compilation of the shopping list and what he could do without.

Adam was feeling exactly the same! They managed to complete the shopping list just before the time limit was up on amendments. The two of them shared the driving as Adam felt up to it but Anna wanted to be sure to give Adam's shoulder a rest. They arrived late afternoon and Adam parked the truck so that the numberplate couldn't be seen, just in case.

Anna gave the kitchen a quick clean over and unpacked the shopping as Adam lit a fire. Anna called the girls and Adam called Maggie. The girls were fine for now, but Maggie stated the beach was awash with journalists, which Maggie sounded excited about. She had been out onto her balcony once to announce that she had no comments to make.

She was hoping they might show it on the TV later, which made both Adam and Anna smile.

The cabin was beautiful and perched on a cliff looking directly out to see, so no beach walkers could view them. They both settled on the sofa exhausted by the travelling. Adam took Anna's hand. "You will be safe here for now." Anna smiled at him as they looked out to sea and let the calm wash over them as night fell.

The moon came up and shone its silvery light across the rolling waves. Anna had purchased fresh tagliatelle and a tomato and mascarpone sauce. She fried up shallots and bacon and doctored the sauce with parmesan, seasoning, white wine, lemon and some mayonnaise. Served with a fresh salad and a nice bottle of New Zealand Sauvignon.

They chatted happily over dinner, with no focus on time as for now time was irrelevant. They both headed for bed when neither of them could keep their eyes open any longer.

Anna was up first the next morning and moved quietly around the lodge to enable Adam to sleep and heal. Anna put the joint of lamb in to slow roast and was sat drinking tea when Adam awoke. "Good morning," stated Anna.

"Good morning, princess," smiled back Adam. It was like being on a honeymoon without the wedding. Anna had set out fresh orange juice, bread, butter, jam and breakfast pastries, along with melon, berries and yogurt. They sat and ate leisurely over breakfast deciding what to do for the day.

They decided to try and find a secluded beach to walk Teddy on. Anna would then prep some vegetables and a potato dauphinoise to go in with the lamb, while Adam cut some wood with his good arm. While the dinner cooked, they decided it would be nice to take a glass of prosecco into the hot-tub and watch the sun set.

"That sounds like my perfect day," stated Anna.

"Mine too," replied Adam. They both cleared away the breakfast and got the layers on to brace the weather. Thankfully, as it was so cold, both could wear hats and scarfs to cover part of their faces aiding the hiding of their identity.

They both enjoyed the beach walk as did Teddy, racing up and down the shoreline. Due to the weather and remoteness of the beach, there were few people to be seen thankfully and as they walked arm in arm, they agreed this would be a good daily ritual. The waves were crashing against the sands as the ocean produced impressively high waves.

They could understand why surfers enjoyed this part of the coast. The tranquility and remoteness of their cottage was magical as they closed the heavy glass doors to the ferocious weather. They really had found a haven in the storm that had been their life over the last few weeks. A life which Adam happened to find himself embroiled in.

Although, he would have preferred a more traditional way of getting to know Anna, he was now beginning to feel it was a blessing in disguise. Anna watched Adam as he stoked the fire as similar thoughts crossed her mind. She had been adamant that she didn't want another man in her life, but this man was different and she felt safe and happy with him.

He accepted her and asked for nothing and put up no ultimatums for his company. They just enjoyed each other.

The cottage had provided lovely soft thick bath robes which they dressed in to get into the hot-tub. Anna hadn't brought a swim suit, Adam was the same so they used the most appropriate underwear. Both tried not to watch the other enter, although a glimpse was unavoidable. They sat in the warm water with a cool glass of prosecco, as they watched the sun set on the ocean.

Adam reached for Anna's hand and drew her to him. They kissed tenderly and Anna felt Adam's arms wrap around her waist as she moved her hand behind his neck, being careful to avoid his injury. Anna felt herself melt as he held her to him. As they parted Adam stroked her cheek and looked into her eyes and she felt herself melt even further.

He had so much love and kindness in his eyes. Anna traced the line of Adam's jaw with her finger and he kissed her nose. "I don't think I could have created a better setting or moment if I had spent years planning it," stated Adam.

"Thank you, Adam, for everything you have done for me." Adam swirled her round in the water.

"The pleasures all mine, well apart being stabbed by a mad ex-husband and having to vacate my home under the cloak of darkness," laughed Adam. Anna splashed him and Adam taken by sunrise, breathed in at that moment and choked. Anna laughed until Adam dunked her. The pair called a truce through giggles and both reached for their glasses.

"This really is like heaven," said Anna. Adam agreed as they both gazed out to sea. The warm water washed away all the stresses and gave them a calmness, which made them both feel at one with the elements. They eventually got out and robed up, quickly making their way to the warmth of the cottage and the log fire.

The smell of the roast filled the cottage, which flooded back childhood memories of the safeness of home. They both felt like they were in some sort of bubble, but what a bubble!

Anna served up the roast and they drank wine, while slowly savoring their meal and talking about family roasts and Christmas days. Adam had Anna in tears of laughter over how Adam's mum would get stressed and his dad would tease her. He would buy her a very inappropriate apron each year.

Once it was one with stockings and suspenders on. His mum would forget she was wearing it and get frustrated when no-one could take her seriously as she chastised her husband for not helping. Eventually, bursting into laughter herself and refusing to continue cooking. A glass of wine later and a little help from Adam's dad and all would be well.

The wine flowed and they cleared up together, eventually settling on the sofa to watch the moon on the waves.

The day couldn't have been more enchanting. As they both felt tired, they decided to head to bed. Both took their time to get dressed for bed. Adam walked round and took Anna in his arms and helped her take off the last of her clothes before lifting her off her feet with a slight wince and laying her on the bed.

He kissed her slowly and she drew him to her, as the hours passed they got to know each other's bodies intimately. They kissed, talked and laughed till sleep took them both. Anna slept in Adam's arms until the morning arrived.

Chapter 11
The New Norm

Adam woke first and decided to let Anna sleep. He showered and stoked up the fire; he unloaded the dishwasher carefully to avoid waking Anna. With such a beautiful view, it didn't seem like a chore. He enjoyed the silence and the feel of the cabin.

Memories of last night filled his heart with feelings he hadn't felt for a very long time. He liked this new norm! He put some of the frozen and ready to bake croissants into the warmed oven and made a pot of tea. He was leant against a beam looking out to sea when Anna walked in. "Morning, princess," he said.

"Morning," replied Anna with a smile, she liked that he had called her princess. No-one had ever called her that or treated her like one, but Adam did. Anna walked over to Adam and he cradled her in front of him so they were both looking out to sea. "I couldn't tire of this view," said Anna.

"Me too," replied Adam as he looked down upon her. They stood for a while enjoying the moment before Anna went for a shower. they ate the croissants with jam, fruit, yogurt and plenty of tea.

"I slept like a baby last night. I can't remember the last time I slept without waking during the night," stated Anna.

"I think you needed a good sleep," he replied. They sat chatting at the table for a while before clearing up after breakfast together.

The two of them had decided that today would be the day to turn on the TV and get updates from Maggie and the girls. Adam called Maggie, who had kept herself informed regarding Mark and his whereabouts. He had remained in custody due to the severity of the charges against him.

His trial was not expected to be for a few months as evidence was gathered and court authorities matched up. It was considered to be a high profile case due to Mark's actions and his position. Maggie stated that the press interest had died down as the whereabouts of Adam and Anna were unknown, but she expected they would return when he and Anna returned, hopefully not on the same scale.

Anna spoke with both her girls. The press had located both of them, but thankfully the local police had acted to turn the press away. Molly and her house mates had been quite excited to have a police protection officer outside her house. The girls had both spoken to their dad and he had apologized.

He had also told them he was having counselling laid on by the police, which was a relief to all; unfortunately, it was too late to reverse the events. Both were asked about media coverage as Adam and Anna had kept the TV off. Both had confirmed that the coverage had died after a couple of days, much to everyone's relief.

Adam and Anna discussed the outcome of the calls and decided to stay in the cottage for the full 3 weeks. They would stay out of sight for the next couple of days in case there were any newspaper types hanging around, then they would treat the last 2 weeks as a bit of a holiday. They both agreed that they deserved it after the ordeal they had been through.

They dressed for a walk on the beach to blow away the cobwebs. Adam and Anna walked the beach for miles until Teddy sat down and refused to go any further. They both laughed and turned back. Adam had volunteered to cook dinner, steak and sautéed potatoes with mushrooms and tomatoes, with a nice bottle of red. "Sounds wonderful," said Anna.

The cabin again offered a calming refuge as they walked in from the winter coastal weather. The wood burner was still ticking over. Adam re-stocked it as Anna poured them a glass of wine, she sat at the kitchen table as Adam cooked. "One more day of seclusion, then we can have a wonder around the local area. Any thoughts on what you want to do?" Anna asked.

"I was going to ask you the same thing," replied Adam. They enjoyed their leisurely dinner and settled on the sofa in front of the fire till their dinner had gone down. Anna suddenly shivered. "Are you cold?" Adam asked.

"No someone must have just walked over my grave," stated Anna.

"You believe that stuff?" Adam asked.

"I'm not sure to be honest," she replied.

"How about we watch the moon over the ocean in the hot-tub?" He asked.

"Sounds amazing!" The hot-tub had a nifty closet by it, like a heated towel rail in a wardrobe to hang towels and robes, which kept them warm and protect by the weather while you were in the hot-tub, greatly appreciated for the few chilly steps back to the cabin.

They both changed into their thick, soft bathrobes and headed to the hot-tub with another glass of wine. "This truly is divine," stated Anna, Adam smiled back as their feet touched and stayed touching, like some sort of footsie, teenagers would play. Anna never expected to be having the feeling of a teenager again and she felt younger than the toll of the last few years at that moment.

They enjoyed the feel of the warm water as they stared out over the ocean and the moon did not disappoint; gleaming a line across the ocean as the stillness of the ocean set like a mill-pool, just before the tide started to ebb back out. A while later, Adam stated he would split a few logs as they were getting low and suggested Anna stayed and enjoyed the hot-tub.

Anna laid back as Adam split the logs with a dull thud and then tossed them into the basket he had brought out and laid by the door with the intention to collect logs before they went in. Anna laid her head back and relaxed, after a while the thuds stopped. Anna looked up.

"Adam, are you still there?" Anna asked, assuming he must have taken the wood into the cabin, but couldn't remember hearing his footsteps and couldn't see him in the cottage.

Anna sat up in the hot-tub as a feeling of panic started to set in. "Adam," she called again. Silence. She started to really worry, trying to reassure herself that there was a simple explanation, but as time passed with no sight or sound of Adam, she couldn't help feeling that something was not right.

She waited and listened for a while longer, not sure what to do.

Where had Adam gone, she tried to make sense of the situation. She thought Mark was in custody, he couldn't be here. All these thoughts rushed through her head as she looked silently for some sort of weapon to defend herself from an unknown onslaught, while trying to tell herself not to be so silly. There was a simple explanation and Adam would appear at any moment.

Anna wasn't sure what to do. She felt venerable in the hot-tub without Adam, but she was also scared to get out. She sat in the hot water and waited, tears started to roll down her face in silence. She couldn't help but expect the worst in those few moments.

From behind, someone grabbed her and plunged her head into the water. Anna already had hold of a wine glass by its stem which she held onto and was smashed in the attack. With all her might, Anna plunged the sharp end of the broken wine glass stem into her assailant.

She heard a cry and felt his pressure on her lessen, enabling her to bring her head above water and gasp for air. Anna scrambled out of the hot-tub and headed for the cabin, hoping the injury would give her enough time.

Anna managed it into the cabin and scrambled to lock the thick glass door. She frantically searched for and found her phone, dialing 999 leaving her phone open and on a live call, in the hope that someone would come. There was only one door into the cabin so Anna checked all the windows and drew all the blinds, then cried as she crouched in a corner of the kitchen.

Teddy had been going crazy in the cabin and now sat in front of Anna on guard. Anna knew Adam was out there, she just hoped he was alive and that help would come soon. She knew whoever was out there wanted her dead. The sound of something heavy hitting the bedroom window sent Teddy into an aggressive attack and Anna let him go.

She heard a yelp and lost all thought of her safety and ran towards where Teddy had yelped. Everything went blank.

Anna came round as she felt herself being dragged. She felt a rope around her ankles pulling her along. She was semi-conscious and not really entirely sure what was happening when she lost consciousness again. Anna again regained consciousness, still with some sort of rope around her ankles. She could hear a man's voice and he sounded annoyed and like he was on the phone.

Anna was on the deck outside the cabin. She scrambled to get the rope off just as her attacker arrived back. "Oh no you don't, little lady." She felt herself being dragged to the edge of the deck, below which was a long drop to the rocks and ocean. Anna scrambled to hold onto something to stop herself being dragged over the edge.

She managed to slow him but she was still heading for the edge; her assailant had dragged her as far as he could. She sensed him move behind her and felt a heavy blow to the back of her head, Anna lost consciousness again.

Adam came too and could hear Anna's panic and a commotion. He was blurry eyed from being struck across the head with a heavy implement while he was chopping wood. He hadn't seen anyone coming so it took him completely by surprise. Adam could see that Anna was being man handled towards the edge of the deck in the dim moonlight and outdoor lights.

He knew he had to act quickly. He picked up the axe and moved silently towards them, just as the assailant was about to push Anna over the edge, Adam brought the axe down on him, without a care to where it hit. He aimed for the center of the assailant in the hope he would hit the moving target and halt him in his tracks.

The axe came down between the man's neck and shoulder, practically severing the arm off; the man fell to the deck. Adam picked up Anna and headed into the cabin.

Adam laid Anna on the couch and made a call to the police, the ambulance were also notified and on their way. Anna was breathing but he had no idea of the injuries she had sustained. He noticed Teddy in a pile on the floor. In his mind, he cried. How could so much pain be tumbled onto such a sweet person.

The ambulance arrived as did the police. The assailant outside was taken away in an ambulance and another was called for Anna. As the ambulance crew attended to Anna, Adam went over to Teddy. He was still breathing. He looked up and saw one of the ambulance crew.

A lady looked over to Adam who had gone over to where Teddy was laying. She walked towards him. "I'm not a vet but can I take a look."

"Please," was all Adam could get out. The paramedic gave him air and checked him over.

"I think he has an internal bleed, possibly caused by a kick or similar." Adam called an emergency vet. After a quick explanation and an assurance that money was no object, they agreed to take Teddy in and one of the officers offered to take him.

Adam and Anna both went to the local hospital in the ambulance. Adam had a gash to his head which needed stitching and Anna had one to the back of her head which needed the same, however she was still unconscious and they were concerned about a brain injury so a brain scan was ordered.

Adam paced the corridors of the hospital, wondering if there was anything that he could have done to prevent this, but he couldn't understand who would have done this or why. He only knew that this must be linked to Mark, but how could he have known that a man in custody could of set this up. How did he find them. Bar locking Anna in a cage, he couldn't have foreseen or prevented this, but he vowed never to let this happen to Anna again.

The results showed that Anna had suffered a slight swelling to a part of her brain. The medical staff put Anna into a medically induced coma, partly so they could avoid any further damage and also to enable them to monitor her progress safely. Adam called Maggie and it all came out. Adam felt the tears roll down his cheeks.

Maggie could hear this in his voice. "I'll call the girls," she said.

"Thank you," was all Adam could muster.

"Don't worry, Adam, it's just a journey, Anna will be fine as will you. Stay safe and strong." Maggie hung up and Adam breathed a sigh of relief. He knew Maggie would work her mother hen charm with the girls and he was so relieved he wouldn't have to make those calls. He wanted to be close to Anna and after the trauma of the night before, he needed some time to understand what had happened and be there for Anna when she awoke.

Adam was gently awoken by a nurse. He had fallen asleep in the chair beside Anna. "Anna's vitals are looking good. We are going to send her for a scan before the doctors decide if she should be woken up. It's going to take some time, we have a room where you could sleep. I promise, me or one of my colleagues will wake you before she is woken."

Adam nodded and was lead to the room which had a single bed and thankfully, a shower, Adam didn't remember falling asleep, he slept for eight hours. It was the first sleep in two days. He awoke with a start and rushed into the hospital corridor to get an update on Anna. Anna was still asleep in her sedated coma, Adam headed for a shower.

Adam arrived at Anna's bedside, hoping they would stop the coma inducing drugs, which should enable her to wake up. He was in for a long wait! The doctors were happy with Anna's recovery and explained that they would reduce the drugs slowly. The nurses explained that it could be days or even weeks before she awoke.

Adam rested his head in his hands. He didn't know how long he had been like that when he felt a hand on his shoulder. He looked up to see Maggie, behind her were Em and Molly. Both rushed to their mother's bedside. A nurse who was attending to Anna reassured the girls and started to explain what was going on. "We'll go get coffee," stated Maggie as she led Adam out of the room.

"I've found out who the awful man that attacked you is. He's an out and out criminal, looking for a quick buck. I suspect Mark hired him with a large financial offer. He's been in and out of prison with charges that range from blackmail to kidnapping. He has absolutely no scruples. Hopefully, he will be locked up for a very long time now."

Adam didn't have the energy to respond. They collected 4 coffees and headed back to the hospital room. As they walked towards the room where Anna was, two police officers approached them. "Are you Adam Williams?"

"Yes, I am," replied Adam.

"I'm afraid we need you to come with us."

"What?" Maggie said. "Don't you realize what this man has been through?"

"I'm sorry, Madam, it's simply routine."

"It's ok, Maggie, I expected this. I attacked a man in defense, but only we know the circumstances. I need to make statements and make sure the police understand what happened." Maggie hugged Adam and watched as he was led away.

Maggie knew he was strong, but what else could be thrown at him. It all felt so unfair. She headed back to the girls.

Chapter 12
The Recovery

Adam arrived back at the hospital unslept and disheveled, he had been interrogated and interviewed all night and finally released without charge. He walked into Anna's hospital room to find Molly asleep on a chair with her head on Anna's bed. It was 6am. Clearly Molly had been there all night.

Maggie and Em had been convinced to head to a local hotel to get some sleep, Molly refused. Adam sat in the other chair in the room and watched Anna and Molly; like mother, like daughter. He fell slightly more in love with the pair. Adam fell asleep in his chair.

Maggie and Em arrived at Anna's hospital room around 9am, both smiled at the sight of Molly and Adam sleeping soundly dedicated to be with their loved one. Maggie silently went to speak with the ward receptionist and secured beds for the both of them nearby.

On waking them, both were handed coffees they had picked up on their way in. The 4 of them sat willing Anna to come round. Adam and Molly looked a state through lack of sleep, both had heavy eyelids and black rims under their eyes. After an hour, Maggie suggested they sleep in the rooms nearby which she explained the ward nurse had organized.

Molly agreed and Em walked her sister to her bed, promising she would wake her with any development. Maggie moved towards Adam. "Come along, young man, you will be no use to her in this state. You need to sleep. We will watch her while you do."

Adam agreed as the nurse who had provided the bed the night before arrived and led him to the small room with a single bed in. "She will be fine," said the nurse as she shut the door to Adam's room. Adam again couldn't remember falling asleep.

Adam again woke with a jolt and headed to Anna's room. Maggie and Em where sat either side of Anna who was still asleep. Maggie took one look at him and reached into her bag, handing him a travel shaving and shower pack. Adam smiled. He moved towards Anna and laid a kiss on her forehead and headed to have a shower.

Molly raced into Anna's hospital room on waking, saddened by no change. Maggie gave her a motherly hug and handed her another travel shower pack and walked her to the shower.

All four were back in the room when Anna blinked and opened her eyes. Everyone leapt to their feet. "It's ok, Anna, you're in the hospital, all is well," said Adam. It took a while for Anna to come round, she was still very dazed drifting in and out of sleep. After a week and many tests, Anna was discharged and the doctors declared that there was no long term damage.

Maggie and the girls had returned home and took Teddy with them. Adam had packed all their things from the cottage into his truck and booked a room at The Seaview Restaurant hotel in Padstow which had a wonderful balcony overlooking the estuary. Adam felt they would be safer in a hotel and Anna could convalesce there before they took the long journey home.

The hotel was owned by Rick Stein, Anna's favorite chef. Adam was chuffed he was able to be able to book a room there, knowing how excited Anna would be to stay there. They could eat in the restaurant without the need to venture out, unless Anna felt up to it. Adam felt being in a public place would be safer.

The intrusion of the press was no longer Adam's concern. Anna was enthralled to be staying at the restaurant, a surprise Adam hadn't let onto Anna until they arrived. The room was beautiful and their private balcony had wonderful views of the estuary below. Adam and Anna spent a relaxed afternoon chatting, looking out across the estuary and watching the comings and goings of the people below.

"This is wonderful, Adam," she stated as she squeezed his hand in delight, excited by the prospect of dinner. She had always wanted to visit Padstow and stay in this hotel, so it was a bit of a dream come true for her. Anna took a long soak in the bath before they both dressed for dinner. Anna still couldn't quite believe where she was!

The smell wafting up from the restaurant greeted them as they headed down the stairs to eat. It was a wonderful combination of hot shells, sweet prawns, fresh fish, lemon, butter, brandy and garlic. It had a sweetness to it promising the delights on the menu, which Anna couldn't wait to view.

They were seated at a lovely table by the window, looking out to the estuary. The waiter handed them the menu and Adam ordered some wine. Anna took a moment to look around the restaurant, in awe that she was actually in Rick

Stein's restaurant. She had been a fan of his for years and had watched all his programs and still did watch them over and over again.

If at home and she wanted the company of the TV, she would always have one of his series on and episode after episode would play through, much to the annoyance of her daughters. Anna found watching them calming and he was always her go to when at a loss for something to watch.

Anna read and re-read the menu. She knew straight away what she wanted for mains, it was the Fruits De Mer—a wonderful selection of shellfish, served on a large three tier platter. "What are you going to go for?" Anna asked.

"Ummm," mulled Adam. "I know what I want for main." They both said Fruits De Mer at the same time and laughed together. They had found that they had so many similar likes, they both decided on the fish and shellfish soup to start.

"If you are going to get a good seafood soup, this has got to be that place," said Anna excitedly. They put down the menus and Anna grinned in anticipation. Adam hadn't quite realized how excited and thrilled Anna would be to be staying and eating here. After all she had been through, Adam was glad he had decided to book this place.

He realized at that moment that he had fallen in love with Anna and he wanted to spend the rest of his life making her happy.

The two of them sipped their wine and Anna looked into Adam's eyes and melted. She didn't think she would ever love again. She had said it, she had fallen in love with Adam and she felt very glad about it. She had thought that she would be spending the rest of her life alone, or in a lonely loveless marriage and here she was feeling like a schoolgirl with a kind man who only seemed to put her happiness first, she had to pinch herself.

Adam leant over and took Anna's hand as he saw a tear well in the corner of her eye. "Are you ok, Anna?" He asked.

"More than happy. I didn't expect to find such happiness again ever, even with all that has happened."

Adam squeezed her hand. "Me neither," stated Adam.

"Me neither." The waiter brought the soup, with fresh, warm sourdough bread and real butter. The soup was indeed amazing, sweet with all the tastes of the sea and a hint of brandy and cream. Adam seemed to breath his in and Anna laughed at him, making Adam slow down. "It's just so good," stated Adam. Anna agreed, still smiling.

The main arrived and was impressive. There was lobster, crab, razor clams, oysters, mussels, prawns, scallops, cockles and two crustations. Anna remembered eating with her father which she hadn't seen on menus for a long time, winkles and whelks.

Anna and Adam chatted and slowly devoured the impressive selection, served with more warm sough dough and the wonderful butter. The process of picking through the shellfish took a delicious amount of time and both of them shared the delights of each different type of shellfish. A warm bowl of water and lemon slices with white cloth napkins was provided for dipping you're fingers in.

All part of the wonderful process of eating such jewels of the sea. Anna sat back and looked up at Adam as she finished, Adam was doing the same. "That was wonderful," she stated. Adam wholeheartedly agreed. They were both full so they skipped desert and ordered a liquor coffee.

They decided to take a walk along the estuary to help their dinner go down. Anna linked arms with Adam as they wondered along enjoying the walk. They stopped to admire the view and watch the goings on. They both turned to each other and Adam leant down to kiss Anna.

It was a long and tender kiss, one that said I'm going to look after you. Anna felt her heart jump a beat, she had never expected this. They headed back to the hotel, stopping at the bar for a G&T, before they headed to their room to enjoy the twinkling view and relax. Adam poured them another G&T, he'd brought supplies from the cottage.

They wondered out onto the balcony to appreciate the view below. Anna stood beside Adam and he put his hand over hers, it was a special spot. Anna shivered and Adam led her inside. They kissed and they both started to undress. Anna could hear Adam's breath become heaver and she felt her pulse rise.

Adam lifted her onto the bed, and they slowly came together in an intense and loving way. Neither had experienced before, an inexplicable love for one another. Anna felt like the world was somewhere else, all that existed was the two of them and the here and now, bliss followed.

The following day took a similar path. Both of them enjoying this little window of time together in such a wonderful seaside town. The following morning, Adam woke before Anna and stood out on the balcony with a cup of tea. The cool air refreshing his sleepy head as he recalled the last few days. He looked back at Anna still sleeping and wondered how he had arrived in such a happy place through such adversity.

Anna must have felt his glance as she opened her eyes and smiled at him, spreading herself across the bed in a morning stretch. She laid and watched him through the glass, wondering what the future would hold. For now, she was happy in this bubble. Adam had booked the hotel for four nights and she intended to make the most of it.

They wandered down to breakfast and took their time to enjoy all the wonderful treats on offer. They both had a full English breakfast followed by yogurt and fruit, croissants and jam, washed down with a pot of tea. They were given the same table by the window and decided to take another walk along the estuary.

The day was one Anna would always remember. They walked and chatted, popped into interesting shops and Anna purchased items for the girls. Adam bought Maggie a hare statue fashioned out of driftwood. They walked, talked and enjoyed the ambiance of what Padstow had to offer. They ate fresh do-nuts and purchased fudge, eventually wandering back to the hotel to sit in the lounge and recover from the chill of the day.

Anna became tired so they returned to the room and Anna took a well needed nap. Adam popped to reception to see if the famous chef was in town during their stay. He would love to arrange a meeting for Anna while they were there. While Adam was relaying snippets of what Anna had gone through and why a meeting would be something, Anna could only dream of the said chef arrived from behind the receptionist, having overheard the conversation.

"Wow, sounds like you've been through the mill," said Rick. "I'd be honored to meet Anna, are you staying in the hotel?" Agreement was made to serve afternoon tea the following day in a more private area of the hotel and Rick would join them as a surprise, afterwards for a glass of champagne.

"Sounds quite exciting," said Rick as he shook Adam's hand while chuckling, before he disappeared into the restaurant kitchen. Adam couldn't believe his luck and again felt grateful for the blessings bestowed on him.

Adam returned to the room to find Anna still asleep. He smiled at the thought of the surprise that awaited her tomorrow. When Anna awoke, she had a long bath while Adam dealt with a few business issues he needed to sort. Anna called the girls again to reassure them she was well and to check they were ok.

Adam called Maggie to check she was also ok. All was good. He didn't want to know about Mark or the other assailant, he would address that when he got home. That evening, they decided to book into a local Chinese restaurant. They wandered to the restaurant and enjoyed a very nice meal in the oriental ambiance.

The staff looked after them and made them feel very welcome. They took the walk back to the hotel. "I really don't want this to end," said Anna. Adam stopped and kissed her on the forehead. "I love you, Anna, and I want you to be a part of my life."

Anna looked up at Adam. "Me too," stated Anna as she squeezed his arm. They walked along they estuary with renewed warmth, in the knowledge that they both shared a deep love for each other. They also both knew that these days were not the normal and sooner or later, they would have to return to some sort of normality.

But for now, now was here in the moment, a holiday, a break from the norm and a time to recover from the traumas and get to know the other person better, the other person that neither of them expected to arrive in their lives.

Adam again woke before Anna. The doctors had said it would take time for her body to fully recover and that sleep was the best form of healing, so Adam was always quiet, trying not to wake her. He again stood on the balcony with a cup of tea enjoying the view and sweet morning air. It gave him time to think, and get used to his deepening love for Anna.

He became angry at what Mark had tried to do, twice! Trying to snuff out her life for his selfish satisfaction. He ticked himself off, now was time for them, he should leave out any thought of that man and with that, he did. Adam made a few business calls from the chill of the balcony, but was glad to get a few factors tied up before Anna awoke.

He turned to see Anna watching him as he finished his last call, he smiled at her and got the same back. He walked back into the warmth of the room and sat on the side of the bed. "You are freezing," Anna said as she engulfed him in the quilt and her legs.

Adam laughed as she practically suffocated him. Once he found a breathing hole, he breezily lifted Anna and moved her so he was propped on his elbow looking down on her. "Morning, princess."

Anna thought that she would never forget these last few days. "Good morning, handsome," she replied.

They went down for breakfast and Adam felt excited about the afternoon tea and Anna's sunrise. They walked along the estuary after breakfast and filled the morning again investigating all that Padstow had to offer. It truly was a magical place with so many wonderful little gems to investigate.

About 1pm, Anna suggested tea and cake. Adam stated that he had organized afternoon tea at the hotel at 3. Anna clapped her hands and jumped up and down. "Ooh, I love afternoon tea," Anna stated. Adam secretly thought, *I think you may love this one more than the average!*

They passed a small shack selling the days catch in small pots. They both purchased a pot each with a selection of shellfish which they doused with vinegar and white pepper and picked at with a cocktail stick as they wandered along. It was enough to fill the gap before afternoon tea without filling them up.

The estuary was again a millpond of turquoise green and aqua blue and the sun was out; jumping its rays off the still water. The gulls were making their familiar sound, laughter was in the air mixing with the clinks and sounds of the boats around the harbor. The sunshine was encouraging people to walk out and enjoy this heavenly corner of England, adding to the happy and care-free feeling of the place.

They wandered back to the hotel to freshen up, ready for their afternoon tea and they walked down just before 3. Adam and Anna were guided to a private corner of the hotel and the afternoon tea was served. It was delicious and both of them enjoyed every morsel. There were cocktail sausage rolls and dainty sandwiches with their crusts cut off, filled with smoked salmon and cream cheese, ham and mustard and egg mayonnaise with cress.

On another level of the three tiered China stand were beautiful scones with jam and clotted cream and an assortment of delicious cakes on the top tier, all washed down with a pot of English Breakfast tea. The famous chef had instructed to be informed when the two had finished their afternoon tea. He arranged for 3 glasses of champagne to be taken out.

Anna looked quizzically at the waitress who placed the glasses down, one in front of Anna, one in front of Adam and another in front of a chair the waitress pulled up to their table. Anna now looked quizzically at Adam. "Are we expecting a guest?"

Adam smiled as Rick approached the table at that very moment and casually said, "Hello, Anna." Anna practically jumped out of her chair and gave Rick a full bear hug.

"I am a massive fan," said Anna.

"Yes, Adam told me," laughed Rick as he sat down in the 3rd chair and raised his champagne for a toast. "To new beginnings," proposed Rick.

The 3 of them all clinked glasses and said in harmony, "To new beginnings."

"I hear you have had a bit of a rough time over the last few weeks, I saw it on the TV," stated Rick. "I'm glad you chose our little hotel for a few days of rest and relaxation. It's an honor to meet you both." They clinked glasses again.

"You too," stated Anna. She could not believe she was in the company of the man she had watched so many times on the TV. They chatted easily about food, travels and Cromer crab of course. The conversation went on longer than intended as Rick and Anna had so much in common.

"Crikey," stated Rick as he checked his watch. "I'd better get back or the chefs will have my guts for garters." He bid them goodbye. He was cooking in the restaurant that evening. He kissed Anna on the cheek. "It was a delight to talk to you," he stated before he shook Adam's hand and headed back to the kitchen. Adam had said very little as Anna and Rick had chattered so enthusiastically about food and their travels.

Anna sat back flabbergasted. "How the hell did you pull that one off?" Anna said.

"I asked," stated Adam simply. Anna lent over and gave him a kiss.

"Thank you," she said gratefully, then sat back in her seat, still awe struck, trying to comprehend what had just happened. They had skipped lunch and had the afternoon tea quite early. Their table for dinner was booked for 9 as Adam knew they would still be quite full from the afternoon tea. They decided to take a drive along the coast and find a nice spot to walk.

They walked for over an hour further up the coast, before heading back to freshen up and to get dressed for the evening meal. Anna was quite excited as she knew Rich Stein was in the kitchen. She never expected he would be actually cooking, let alone meet him.

They bathed and showered leisurely. Adam poured them a G&T while they sat and chatted in a couple of comfy chairs overlooking the estuary. "What an amazing day!" Anna exclaimed. Adam smiled back at her, he was pleased he had been able to make one of her dreams come true.

Tonight was to be their last night. Anna was well recovered and they would make the journey home tomorrow. It was over a 6 hour drive so they had decided to stop at an old cozy coaching inn for an overnight stay on the way. Adam's shoulder was still not completely healed and he refused to let Anna drive.

They headed down for dinner with the sweet smell of shellfish in their nostrils. They were seated in their usual table in window overlooking the estuary and handed the menu. Adam ordered champagne as it was their last night and they perused the menu. Anna looked into Adam's eyes and couldn't quite believe where she was and how life had moved on.

It had been horrendous and amazing; tonight was going to be bitter sweet. Adam chose the scallops to start and Anna chose oysters. They both opted for the lobster for their main and each offered and shared a taste of each other's first course. The evening passed with chat, laughter and amazing food.

Adam thought he couldn't be happier. He had an amazing lady in Anna and he knew he was in love with her. Anna was thinking the same. The restaurant buzzed with happy chat, laughter, chinking of glasses and a wonderful smell of seafood, hot shells, brandy, cream and butter.

The lights twinkled in the estuary and the two of them felt a connection which could never be broken. A love to protect and keep the other safe and happy. They smiled, laughed, chattered in a place they felt safe, their room was upstairs and the wine flowed. Neither would forget this evening or the love they had developed for each other.

They headed for bed after coffee and spent a happy couple of hours chatting upstairs looking out onto the twinkly lights of the estuary. "We should come back here," said Anna.

"I totally agree," stated Adam. They both climbed into bed and made love tenderly before they slept soundly and happily with the sound of the estuary coming through an open window.

The following morning, they woke and packed before heading down to breakfast. "I am really going to miss this place," said Anna.

"Me too, princess, me too." Anna's heart still skipped a beat whenever he called her that. This time last year she had felt unloved, middle aged and worn down by life. She had never been treated or made to feel like a princess, but Adam did and she loved him all the more.

They ate breakfast leisurely looking out on the wonderful view, with full bellies, they headed back to their room to collect their luggage. As they packed the car, they both looked back at the hotel and the wonderful view. Adam walked over to Anna and gave her a hug.

He knew it would be difficult for them both to return to the small seaside town of Cromer with all of the gossips which no doubt would be circling, but he also knew she needed some normality and the trip home was the first step.

Chapter 13

The journey home was uneventful and soon passed as they chatted. They stopped at an old coaching Inn and had a nice meal in the old bar beside a crackling log fire. The old lodge was quaintly English, with low beamed ceilings and a large polished wooden bar.

The following morning, they had 4 hours left to travel and would stop half way for breakfast. Adam patted Anna's leg as they approached Adam's cottage. Both had agreed that for now, Anna would stay with him. The two of them unpacked the car and headed in, eager to avoid engaging with anyone who might come by.

It was mid-afternoon when they arrived home. Once unpacked, Adam lit the fire and they decided on a Chinese takeaway. "I'm so glad to be back with this view," said Anna. Adam nodded in agreement as they sat together on the sofa, looking out to sea. The doorbell rang to announce the arrival of their evening meal.

Anna laid the table and got the plates out of the oven where they had been warming, while Adam went down to collect the delivery. Both enjoyed the crispy chilli beef, sweet and sour king prawns, special fried rice, noodles and mushroom fu young and prawn crackers. Both of them sat back feeling well fed.

They had enjoyed the delights of the seafood restaurant but a dirty take away was very welcome in the familiar place that was Adam's home. They cleared up and headed for the sofa. Before they knew it, they were both asleep on the sofa. Adam woke at 2am and gingerly carried Anna to bed.

The next morning, the two of them headed over to Maggie's to pick up Teddy. As they approached Teddy raced towards them, having been stood with Maggie on the deck while she waited for their arrival. Teddy was super excited to see them, racing between and around them as they stepped towards Maggie's.

The two of them were welcomed with hugs and ushered into the house which had a welcoming fire burning. Maggie already had a bottle of prosecco on ice with three glasses on a silver tray. "A welcome home celebration," stated Maggie as she handed the bottle to Adam to open.

The 3 settled down as Anna filled Maggie in on their trip. Maggie as usual had been digging; she had found out the person who attacked them was a well-known thug who had spent time in the same prison that Mark was residing in, culminating in a theory that Maggie had created.

Anna hadn't wanted to think about it but knew that her time in court would come. She had given her statements and was happy to leave it to the authorities. Adam sensed this and quickly changed the subject. Maggie was soon filling them in on all the local gossip as they nibbled on the spread Maggie had laid out and sipped their prosecco.

After leaving Maggie's, they wandered over to Anna's cottage to check on it, then onto the café, all was well. Anna felt a shiver go down her spine as she entered, remembering the evening of the attack. Adam gave her a hug as he saw her shiver. Anna was determined to get the café back up and running and fill it with happy memories again.

They headed back to Adam's via Harry's and a cup of tea. "I've missed my lunches, Anna," said Harry.

"They will be back up and running soon enough," smiled Anna. She had missed Harry and was looking forward to getting back to normal.

"These is no hurry, Anna, take all the time you need," stated Harry smiling at Anna, relived that all seemed well.

The two headed back to Adam's along the beach. "I've missed this," stated Anna.

"Me too," agreed Adam. They walked back arm in arm as Teddy ran around the beach. A few of the locals had stared at them, which they both expected, but thankfully, the media hadn't picked up on the attack in Devon, so there was no media around. Anna had organized a grocery delivery and put on a beef stew, which could blip for a few hours while the two of them got organized and made the calls they needed to.

Adam was aware that both Anna and himself still needed to take it a bit easy, so no plans were made for the next few days, while they eased back into their new normal routine.

A couple of days had passed when Adam suggested. "How about I take you out to dinner at the Rocky Bottom, considering our last trip was a little spoilt?" Adam asked.

"Sounds perfect," replied Anna. "It would be lovely," she said as she smiled up at Adam, who promptly laid a kiss on her lips. Adam had booked a secluded table by the window, looking out to sea. The setting was beautiful, a candle on the table flickered its ambient light. The restaurant had floor to ceiling windows and the moon was shining bright.

They decided to share two starters of spiced chilli and salt squid and popcorn cockles; both of which were delicious. They went for the sharing seafood platter for mains. As they picked through their platter, Adam asked, "Do you have any plans regarding the café yet?"

"Well," mused Anna. "I want to open up in a couple of weeks. I need to do a clean out as it's been empty for a while and plan my deliveries and so forth. What about you?" Anna asked.

"Well, I've decided to stick around here for a while just till things settle down. It also means I can help you set up the café. How about we head to the café in the morning and make a plan of action?"

"Sounds good," said Anna.

The following morning, the 2 of them headed out to the café as planned and started on a few elements, while putting a plan into action. It actually wasn't too bad. Anna cleaned some of the surfaces and put everything through the dishwasher to freshen it up. Adam tidied up the outside, assessing which blankets needed washing and re-stocking.

Adam had lit the wood burning stove and stocked up the wood to warm up the chilli café. After the 5th walker asked when the café would re-open, Anna put a sign in the window to confirm the re-opening date. She was confident with the work they had done today and was keen to get back to normal.

Adam Knocked up a sign which he hammered into the sand a little way from the café. They both sat by the log burner and Anna got them a cold beer out of the fridge, they clinked bottles. "Good job done," said Anna. "The place is nearly ready." Anna just needed to place her orders and decide on her menus.

The 2 of them headed back to Adam's to shower. Both of them had showered and were sat in Adam's living room on the comfy sofas as the wood burner crackled. "It's good to be getting back to normal," stated Anna.

"Agreed," said Adam as he pulled her in for a cuddle, breathing in the sweet smell of her freshly showered body. They ate a simple pasta dish before bed beaconed and they both fell asleep soundly and deeply. The next day was a Sunday.

Molly and Em were coming over for a roast and it was the first time Anna would be cooking it at Adam's, so she had a bit of apprehension, but knew all would be well in such a well-equipped large kitchen.

Anna awoke and put the leg of lamb into a hot oven which she turned right down, for a low and slow cook. Anna pottered and made tea, while setting up some breakfast nibbles. Anna hadn't noticed Adam come to the top of the stairs, as she pottered around the kitchen. Adam leant against the top of the banister with his arms folded, watching Anna as she happily moved around the kitchen.

When Anna felt his presence and looked up, he was already smiling at her. "What are you up to?" Anna asked.

"Just enjoying the view, princess." Adam walked over and lifted her off her feet for a kiss.

"Good morning," stated Anna.

"Yes, it is," replied Adam. They enjoyed a leisurely breakfast before they walked Teddy along the beach. There seemed more walkers that morning. Both Adam and Anna saw the stares and heads coming together in whispers. Adam

139

had hoped this would not have been the case, but he had feared it all the same.

"Can we head home now?" Anna asked. Adam could hear the anxiety in her voice as he guided her back to the safe haven of his beach house, now annoyed at the thoughtlessness showed by some of his community.

Once safe inside, Adam hugged Anna to him. He felt the dampness of her tears on his chest. *Dam you, Mark,* he thought. "One day at a time, princess, one day at a time." Anna smiled up at him and he kissed her on the lips before hugging her again.

Anna busied herself with preparing the roast, the girls were due at 2pm for a late lunch. Adam called Maggie and explained what had gone on. Maggie had conveyed that unfortunately the events of the past few months had stirred an interest in the local gossips, coupled with the fact that Adam was considered one of Norfolk's most eligible bachelors.

She feared it was only a matter of time until the press came snooping again, if the gossips need for detail were not fed. Adam feared that their plans for the next few weeks may need to change, but for now it was family time, so he said goodbye to Maggie and started to prepare for the arrival of the girls.

As soon as the girls arrived, the mood changed. Molly was her usual giggling self. It seemed that mishaps on the beach were drawn to her view, or it may have just been that her observations and commentary made them all the more amusing, either way, her fits of giggles which sometimes reduced her to roll around on the floor, unable to get her words out, made everyone smile, along with her babbled recollections between fits of giggles, along with charades of re-enactment which had everyone laughing.

The smell of the roast filled the house and Adam looked after the setting of the table and ensuring everyone had their refreshments topped up. Molly was staying over at Adam's, and Em and her fiancée had taken a couple of days off and were staying at Anna's.

Adam had set the table to make it extra special. He had laid a thick cream tablecloth with a rich checked runner which matched his furnishing; cream and checked napkins, folded to sit his finest cutlery within. He had asked the local florist to deliver 3 low flower bowls, filled with white and lime flowers, a combination he knew Anna liked.

He laid out water and wine glasses, along with all the condiments in small glass lidded bowls, with tiny spoons. There were also two sets of small pewter salt and pepper pots in the shape of stag heads. As Adam finished, Anna arrived and laid her hand on the base of his back. He instinctively turned and kissed her on the forehead.

They both purveyed the table, unaware of the glances being exchanged behind them. "It looks amazing, Adam, who knew you had such a flair for table settings," teased Anna. Adam playfully squeezed her and laid a kiss in her hair, again noted by their guests. "Dinner is all set and holding in the oven, I'm just waiting on the meat to rest," stated Anna.

"Perfect, let's sit for a pre-dinner drink, before we serve up," replied Adam.

The 5 of them sat and chatted, anticipating the delights they would soon be tucking into, happy to be back together as a family after all the trauma of the last few months. Anna went back to the kitchen to serve up all the dishes. Adam had an impressive range of Denby serving dishes with lids, which Anna was enjoying using.

He also had a huge range with warming draws which made cooking the roast a delight. Anna laid the food out while Adam poured the wine and water. Everyone seated themselves around the table. "I have been dreaming of this, Mum," said Molly eagerly helping herself to large spoonful's of what was on offer, between gulps of red wine. "Nice wine, Adam," she said.

Adam smiled and caught Anna's amused roll of the eyes before she bestowed a look of sheer love on her daughter. "You are such a heathen," scoffed Em with a similar smile and roll of the eye. Molly just flashed a grin at Adam and continued in the same vain.

Adam couldn't help but let out a belly laugh, which was soon reciprocated by the others. "Welcome to the family," laughed Em. Anna held up her glass. "May this be the first of many!" They all clinked glasses and agreed.

Anna had laid on a wonderful spread of roast lamb, mashed and roast potatoes, carrots and sprouts, cauliflower-cheese and red cabbage, not forgetting the Yorkshire puddings and peas. Anna's daughters had their favorites and would ask, "Where is?" if anything was missing, so she had learnt what had to be produced for the roast to qualify it as official.

She would now add cauliflower-cheese and red cabbage to that list. Adam watched as the family happily chatted and teased each other. He had always wanted children and thought that was lost to him, but here he was, happier than he could have ever wished for. He caught Anna watching him, she smiled and mouthed a thank you. Adam raised his glass slightly and winked at her. Regardless of what was going on outside, the strength and love of this family would always prevail.

The following morning, Adam was up first after leaving the 3 girls chatting and reminiscing late into the night before. He put the kettle on and went to open the curtains, relieved to see no obvious signs of the press. He made a pot of tea and put on some coffee, before lighting the fire.

Molly was next up. She skipped across the lounge to her favorite spot, followed closely by Teddy. "Morning, Adam," she sang as she launched herself into the air and landed ungracefully in the comfy chair overlooking the beach, Adam smiled, although he should discourage the treatment of his expensive and carefully chosen furniture, he couldn't help but be amused and he was glad that Molly could feel so at home. He was sure these were feelings held by parents across the land. He started on the breakfast table, putting down a jug of orange juice, pastries etc.

It wasn't long before Molly was in hysterics. "Why don't these people get it, the wave goes out, then comes back in," with that Molly dramatically fell of her chair in fits of laughter, taking Teddy with her. "The oldie just got it, oh my, she's down…" between fits of laughter, Molly managed, "she can't get up…the old guy now…another waves hit…"

With that Anna arrived and went over to see what was causing her daughter such amusement. "Oh my," said Anna, "it's like the keystone cops down there. There is a whole group of them trying to get the couple up, all getting drenched in the process and the lady just kept being engulfed by the next wave, whooshing her around like a beached whale." By now, Molly had completely lost it and could no longer talk.

"We should take them some towels," stated Anna.

"I think in the circumstances we should lay low," stated Adam as he arrived to take a look at the goings on. He had been laughing at Molly's reaction as he was setting up the breakfast. "Oh dear," stated Adam with a chuckle. Eventually, the couple were helped up and led away by some kind locals.

Molly spent the rest of the morning bursting into fits of giggles as the images popped back into her head.

Chapter 14
One Step at a Time

Molly was tasked with walking the dog to discourage the gossips. Maggie had been invited over for the evening. Em and her fiancée also came over as Molly and Em were due to go home the next day, rather than cooking a meal, Anna and Adam laid on a buffet with all the things the girls enjoyed.

Of course Anna made too much so both of the girls could take a stack home. They had a very enjoyable evening, chatting and laughing. During the evening, Molly asked. "So you two, I take it you are an item?" She stated, staring at Anna and Adam in turn.

Molly had asked what everyone else dare not. There was a long pause before Anna spoke. "Yes, we are indeed. We didn't intend it to happened, it just did and I am very happy."

"Well, I for one are very happy for you both," stated Maggie.

"What about you girls?" Anna asked.

Molly piped up first. "Whatever makes you happy, Mum. I like Adam," she stated.

"Why thank you, Molly, the feeling is mutual," said Adam smiling, if slightly embarrassed. All eyes were now on Emily.

Anna spoke again. "I know it must be hard for you as it hasn't been that long since your dad and I separated, especially with what has happened." There was another pause before Emily spoke.

"I know that it hasn't been that long, Mum, but in real terms, it's been years. We could see how Dad was making you feel. Since you moved here and met Adam, you've got your sparkle back, so I'm happy for you both."

There was another pause before Maggie raised her glass for a toast, "To new beginnings!" Everyone raised their glasses and toasted. The matter was settled much to Adam and Anna's relief.

"While we are discussing matters," stated Anna, "we need to talk about your dad's trial which is only 6 weeks away, it will no doubt stir up press interest again. Thankfully, the press haven't been snooping recently, but once the trial starts and the details come out, it may start all over again. Plus myself, Maggie and Adam will most likely be called to give evidence, you may be too."

This time Em spoke first. "He is my dad, but I can't forgive him for what he tried to do…twice! He is, or was, a police-officer and therefore knows the law better than anyone. I am sure he will receive the justice he deserves and I hope he gets help while there. Regarding the press, we have dealt with it before and we will do it again."

"Ditto," stated Molly as she jumped up for another plateful.

"Who's up for a game of cards," stated Maggie, keen to lighten the mood. "I think a small wager may make it a little more exciting!"

"I agree," stated Adam. "I'll get the cards." Anna topped up everyone's drink and a competitive night of cards commenced. Any talk of the trial, the press, Adam and Anna's relationship and what had happened was put to bed, for now.

The next morning, the girls packed the car to make their way home, laden with provisions left from the buffet. Teddy darted about between them all as hugs and kisses were exchanged. Adam hugged Molly goodbye and was surprised by the bear hug he received back.

"Thanks for looking after, Mum," she said, "I'm here for you too, Molly, you have my number, no matter what, just call me; that goes for your sister too." Molly gave Adam another hug and the smile she flashed him as she got in the car melted his heart, he suddenly felt very protective of the two girls. Adam and Anna stood together as they waved them goodbye.

Adam gave Anna a loving squeeze, he knew how much she hated saying goodbye to the girls, strangely he felt a sadness too. "Come on," said Adam. "Let's walk Teddy along the beach, blow the cobwebs away and bugger the gossips." Anna smiled and agreed. They went in to wrap up for a blustery walk.

Thankfully, the walk was uneventful. There didn't seem to be too many stares or whispers. Maybe Molly walking Teddy and a few days passing had settled the gossips tongues. They walked by Harry's and stopped for a cuppa. No mention was made to open the café, however Anna was feeling that it may be time.

They popped into the café to check on it. The preparation they had made meant it was ready to open. "Shall we light the fire to dry off the damp and have a beer or two?" Anna asked.

"Good plan," said Adam. He felt she needed something to keep her occupied and no doubt she would potter while they were there. Adam lit the inside log burner while Anna did indeed potter around; dusting, polishing and moving stuff around, before she fetched 2 beers from the fridge and went to sit by the log burner.

Adam joined her. After a few moments of enjoying the warmth from the fire and watching the waves, Adam spoke, "Now that I don't have any contracts in the pipeline, how about we open up the café together. I can work on the odd jobs which need doing, maybe we could even make some improvements. If you need any help, I'll be here and if we have any press snooping about, I can see them off."

Anna thought for a few moments before she looked up at Adam with a beaming smile. "I would like that very much!" Adam leant down and kissed her.

"That's settled then." They chinked their bottle together as both of their thoughts turned to plans for the opening and future of the café.

The café was due to open on Saturday, 2 days away. "We are ready," declared Anna. "Other than some food prep, I can order all the provisions today and do the cooking prep tomorrow. I need to pop over to the café to check on stock before I make the orders," said Anna.

Adam kissed her. "Whatever makes you happy." He had seen the excitement in her since they decided to open. He thought it would be good for both of them, they could also see off the gossips together. Anna jumped up raring to go, Adam smiled and went off to load any tools he might need over the couple of days.

Anna packed up anything she might need today, which wasn't much as the café held most of what she needed and the cooking would be left to tomorrow. An hour later, they headed out to the café. Anna checked the stock and made a list of all she would need, then called in the orders.

All of her suppliers were glad to hear from her and wished her the best, which made Anna feel more like a part of the community again. *It felt good to be active and moving forward again,* she thought. The café would only be open for Saturday and Sunday, until the normal café opening hours resumed again on Wednesday.

Anna didn't need too much, with few people knowing about the opening, she didn't expect to be too busy. She did, however, expect the gossips to arrive on Wednesday, so she intended to encourage her locals to reserve a table for the following week, just in case. After they both felt the days tasks were completed, they headed over to Harry's to let him know, finalized plans. Needless to say he was very pleased.

Maggie was also aware and had already reserved her favorite table for each day of the first two weeks of opening. She would stay for lunch as she knew her presence would keep the locals in check, plus she didn't want to miss a thing!

The following day, Anna was busy making sausage rolls, cakes and quiches. Adam was working on internal maintenance, taking advantage of the fact that there were no customers. The signs seemed to be keeping passes by at bay, other than a wave and or thumbs up.

Anna enjoyed having Adam around and Adam felt the same. Adam was also enjoying being chief taster of anything which came out of the oven. Adam had also stocked up on wood for both wood burners and prepped them for lighting the next day.

By mid-afternoon, they were done and both sat down with a beer, clinking to confirm a job well done. They headed back to Adam's, happy in the knowledge that today had been some sort of normal.

The following morning, they set off for the café early so Anna could make up the sandwiches and put the sausage rolls through the oven. Adam lit both the fires and set up the outside benches and tables, along with rugs and hurricane candles. Anna smiled at Adam finding his inner Zen as he arranged the tables, moved the condiments, rugs and candles around till it was just so.

As before, they were going to open Wednesday to Sunday from 10 till 2. As this was Saturday, they were easing into it with just 2 days to open. As it approached 10am, there were a few locals hanging about outside as Anna opened the door. All were friendly and greeted Anna like an old friend.

"We are so pleased to see you open. We have missed this so much," said her first guest. A sentiment that most of her customers conveyed. Adam busied himself but was ready to help whenever needed. Some of the locals gave a knowing smile at the sight of Adam and greeted him in a similar way.

"Glad to see you here, Adam, looking after our Anna. Such a terrible business," said one. There was the expected initial rush, however once the few tables were filled, it quietened down and Anna soon settled into her usual flow, chatting with her customers and making sure everyone had all they needed. Thankfully, there were no signs of the press or the gossip mongers, just her usual customers.

Most had taken her advice and booked up slots for the next couple of weeks much to Anna's relief. For one, it meant she knew her café would be filled not allowing press or gossips to encamp, and for two, she knew she had friends round her. She thought her customers were of the same mind and she was grateful for that.

Harry arrived at 12 for his lunch and then resumed his front of house position until close, meaning Adam was ousted to do outside maintenance, which he bowed to with a smile. The day sped by, many of the locals purchasing items to take home. "We have missed your cooking, Anna," said more than one.

Thankfully, Anna had prepared for this and had plenty of back-ups for such an eventuality and to make sure she would be fully stocked the following day. Maggie arrived late on with a chilled bottle of bubbly. She helped Anna clear down and the 4 friends enjoyed a celebratory glass in the now quiet café. "Well done the 2 of you," stated Maggie.

Harry agreed. "You got back on the horse and it didn't bolt!"

"I'll drink to that," said Anna as they clinked glasses again. Anna felt blessed to have such amazing people around her. The following day went in a similar fashion. Anna was glad to close up at the end of the Sunday and heaved a sigh of relief that it had gone without a hitch. Adam noticed and walked over to her.

"I know it took a lot of courage to open this place up, but I think it was the right thing to do." Anna gave him a hug and buried her head into his chest. As she looked up she stated, "Thank you, Adam, for all your help and support, It made it much easier."

"I quite enjoyed myself, even if Harry did banish me to outside maintenance."

Anna laughed. "He does like his position of Maître D!" They closed up and headed home, both of them were looking forward to a couple of days out of the limelight.

Wednesday morning arrived and both Anna and Adam were nervous. They arrived early and unloaded the food Anna had prepared back at Adam's. At 10am, the locals who had booked arrived and the morning seemed to go without a hitch. Adam was outside working on some ideas.

They had to extend the deck and provide additional cover from the elements. Just after lunch, a group of 4 ladies walked in. Anna didn't recognize them and they were a little too well dressed to be beach walkers. Anna became nervous, Adam had noticed the said customers too and the change in Anna.

Harry also had noticed and looked concerned. It was 1pm though and thankfully they would close in an hour. The ladies ordered drinks and snacks and then started to take photos of the food with their phone. Anna was becoming increasingly nervous, the last thing she needed was any social media coverage.

Adam had noticed too, along with the fact that the ladies seemed to now be turning their camera phone onto the interior of the café. They were also filming Anna when she wasn't looking. Harry had also noticed too and decided to play the overly friendly host. He pulled his chair up to the ladies table and stated talking to them, much to the ladies disdain.

Within 10 minutes, the ladies had left and no further images had been taken. Anna's heart sank, she felt like a backward step had been taken and she dreaded what the ladies visit might stir up.

Anna closed the door and flipped the sign at 2. She went over to Harry. "Thank you, Harry, hopefully they won't be back!"

Harry clasped her hands in his. "You are tough, you can take the rough with the smooth. Keep your chin up, don't let the buggers grind you down."

"Thanks, Harry," said Anna with a hug. Harry smiled and bid them goodbye. "Same time tomorrow," he said with a wink and a smile as he headed home. Adam went over to Anna and gave her a hug.

"We have to expect that it won't be all plain sailing, but you have this and you have me and many others by your side." Anna smiled up at him. "Beer," she said.

"Do bears," Adam started.

"Thank you, Adam," Anna interrupted with a smile.

Anna was glad to be back within the safety of Adam's home later that afternoon. As soon as the doors were closed and locked, something they did on auto pilot now, Anna went and changed while Adam lit the fire and poured them a glass of wine each. Adam was already sat on one of the comfy sofa's looking out to sea, enjoying the sound and warmth of the crackling fire as the last light of the day set on the ocean.

Anna let herself fall into the comfort of the sofa beside him, heaving a sigh of relief. "Hard day, princess."

"Don't even ask," she laughed giving her neck and shoulders a stretch. Adam leant over and picked up a glass of wine and handed it too Anna. "Thank you," she replied with a smile, "I am so glad to be here right now."

"Me too," stated Adam. Anna took a sip and let the days stresses melt away. She did not want to think about tomorrow or anything else for that matter.

They ate a simple and relaxed supper of salmon, new potatoes and minted green beans and peas. Anna couldn't help but whizz up a nice sauce with mayo, lemon and capers. "Encourage able," Adam had teased. They ate at the dining table purely because it was closer to the fire.

They ate and chatted over another glass of wine, before a quick clear up and back to their relaxed place on the sofa. About 8pm, the silence of the crackling fire was interrupted by Adam's phone ringing. It was Maggie.

Anna watched as Adam slowly paced. She could see his shoulders drop as he sighed, listening to what Maggie had to say. Adam thanked Maggie and hung up. Adam turned to Anna.

"The women that visited the café have put out some footage of you and the café on their social media, adding their own spin on the situation. It will probably stir up the press and other potential gossips, especially as the trial is only a couple of weeks away," stated Adam.

"I'm not surprised," stated Anna as she got up and headed to pour another drink. "I want to keep the café going somehow," stated Anna. "Being busy keeps me sane," she added. Adam walked over to give her a hug and Anna laid her head against his chest. She was annoyed that Mark had caused this and continued to affect her life.

Adam lifted up her chin and looked into her eyes. "Maggie has offered to run the café tomorrow with my help. She probably wants a bit of the action, you know what she's like." Anna smiled. "We will work something out," stated Adam. Anna managed a small smile and rested her head back on his chest.

The following morning, Anna was up early cooking off and making up all the offerings for the café. Once all packed and ready to go, Maggie arrived, Adam and Maggie then headed off to the café. Anna slumped onto the sofa, frustrated. After about half an hour, she ticked herself off and got to work on tomorrow's bakes.

She decided to produce a special of the day, something easy for Maggie to serve up. Tomorrow would be scotch eggs. She had already put her order in with the supplier the night before and had added to it this morning. She also had sandwich boxes she would use to pack ready-made sandwiches in, again to make life as easy as possible for Maggie.

Just before 3pm, Adam and Maggie walked in. Anna was eager for an update. No press had turned up but there were e few never seen before guests, of a similar age and demographic to the ladies from yesterday. The three of them decided that for the next week, Anna would stay away from the café and continue to produce all the food from Adam's place.

They would review this the following week. The week whizzed by as Anna got into the swing of cooking and baking from Adam's, with the radio on for company and tea on the balcony watching life go by on the beach. By all accounts, her specials were going down well and Anna was adding to the offerings each day, enjoying producing them.

She had added pasties, pies, donuts, cakes and new quiche combinations. When the week was up, they decided Anna would go back to running the café with the help of Adam as a just in case. Anna, Maggie and Adam were all due to give evidence in the following week, so Anna decided to close the café for two weeks, hoping that the trial would be finished by then.

Adam helped Anna close the café up the following Sunday. She had already added notification of the two week closure and had informed all her regulars, who were all very supportive and wished her well. The morning of the trial arrived and Anna had to give evidence first.

Adam and Maggie were called on the same day, but there was no saying when they would be called and they had been informed that their call may roll into the next day, and they may also be re-called. All 3 of them had decided to book into the Maids Head Hotel in Norwich for a couple of nights, just in case. It was just round the corner from the court and the hotel itself would offer them some protection from the press.

As they pulled up to the court, Adam squeezed her leg. Anna smiled at him. She had been dreading this day and here it was. They were all sat in a small room close to where the trial was being held. There was a drinks dispenser and Adam had fetched them all one; the taste of which left a lot to be desired, but it was a needed distraction.

A couple of hours in Anna was called. She hugged both Adam and Maggie before she was lead into the court room. Adam had felt the tremor of Anna's nervousness. As she entered, she saw the judge sat in the center of the bench and the solicitors at their benches. She was lead to the left and ushered up the steps to the witness box.

As she was stepping into the box, she glanced to her right and there was Mark in the glass clad dock. He had his head bent forward. He looked different, frail almost and for a fleeting moment Anna felt sorry for him, before she was addressed by the clerk of the court. Anna had read through her statements while she had waited and that had been difficult for her to revisit.

She was now being cross questioned by Mark's defense. Mark had pleaded not guilty by diminished responsibility. Anna was on the stand for nearly an hour. The defense had tried to claim that she had taunted Mark, causing his rage, which thankfully the prosecution quickly quashed this as untrue, which it was. Anna was finally lead back to the waiting room where Maggie and Adam were, Adam went straight over to her and hugged her to him, at which point the strength Anna had maintained in the courtroom, left her and she burst into tears.

Adam was called next. He had never really got a good look at Mark as the events between them had happened so quickly. Adam couldn't help glaring at Mark as he felt the anger in him raise. He noticed Mark sit up as he entered the court, the two of them exchanged glances. Adam was cross examined and then lead back to the waiting room.

Half an hour later, a clerk arrived to say that that case had been adjourned till the morning, all 3 of them gave a sigh of relief. Adam had seen the press in the court room so briefed the girls for a swift exit and entry to the car which went quite smoothly. Back at the hotel, Anna had a soak in the bath and Adam headed down to reception to book them a secluded table for dinner.

Being so close to the courts meant the staff were used to dealing with such eventualities and booked them onto an appropriate table. The doorman at the front of the hotel were also used to dealing with the press. However, sometimes the press would book into the hotel and Adam was informed of this.

Dinner went without a hitch. If there were any press in the hotel, the positioning of their table meant they were not overlooked. The 3 friends chatted happily over dinner, avoiding any talk of the trial. Adam and Anna were intent on putting it behind them as soon as it was over.

The following morning, the 3 of them headed over to the court. Maggie was called mid-morning and by all accounts entertained the court even producing several waives of laughter. Shortly after Maggie returned to the waiting room, the court clerk arrived to announce that at this point they were no longer required and they were free to go.

Rather than stay another night in the hotel, they headed back to the coast and the sanctity of their beach houses, none of them wanted to remain for the verdict. They were all happy to be informed by telephone.

The following morning, the expected press were camped outside both Adam's and Maggie's homes. "I should imagine they will be here until after the verdict." Which they were. The verdict was read that Friday and Mark was charged with attempted murder amongst other things. Mark received a custodial sentenced totaling 14 years, which would be reviewed to ensure he did not present any danger to Anna, should he be released.

On receiving this news, Anna called the girls. They had visited their dad in custody but did not want to see him in court. Both girls were saddened by the news, but had expected it. Anna and Adam had put a statement together to read to the press outside. The newspapers had reported the proceeding of the trial so they didn't have much left to add, other than to ask they give them some space and allow them to get back to normal.

Thankfully, within a couple of days, they were yesterday's news and the press moved on. Maggie, on the other hand, had appeared on the local evening news, portraying her flamboyant version of events, which had made Adam and Maggie laugh. She had got her moment in the limelight, which Adam and Anna were glad to give up.

Maggie had stated that after her filming. "I am unable to walk down the beach or through the town without being stopped by all and sundry. I feel like a local celebrity!"

"You always have been, Maggie," laughed Adam. Both Adam and Anna were glad that Maggie was quenching the locals interest in them, that way they could get back to normal sooner.

Chapter 15
The New Normal, or Is It?

A few weeks after the trial, Adam had taken a job in London and would be away for a few weeks, coming back every other weekend. Anna had moved back to her beach house and the café was open and flourishing. Anna was enjoying her freedom again even though she did miss Adam, she was glad to get back to normal.

Anna had become a welcomed local and after all that had happened, the locals had taken her to their hearts and she felt that every day. The café was becoming a go to destination for many. Anna had also started making and selling ketchups, jams, pickles and numerous other items which her customers could buy to take home.

Some were even buying them to give as gifts, making Anna think if this could be something she could sell online. Anna loved to cook and all the new creations Anna was cooking up were keeping her energized and busy. Molly and Em were coming up on Sunday and staying for the bank holiday Monday.

Adam had offered his house for Em and her fiancé, and Molly would stay with Anna. They had booked a table at their favorite restaurant, the Rocky Bottom, for Sunday evening and invited Maggie and Harry.

They were seated looking out to sea and the owner was looking after them himself as special guests, as requested by Adam. The friends laughed and chatted, finally able to relax after the turmoil of the last few months.

The following day was a relaxed affair, drinking tea on the deck and walking Teddy on the beach. Maggie had invited them to join her for lunch and Pimm's at her house. Molly, Anna and Teddy meandered along the beach towards Maggie's late morning. It was a gloriously sunny day with a light breeze. "You've done well for yourself, Mum," said Molly. "I'm happy for you."

"Thanks, Mols," said Anna as she hugged her. As usual, Maggie had laid on an amazing spread of canapes, sandwiches and sausage rolls amongst other things. The afternoon slipped by as the 5 of them chatted, ate and sipped.

A few days later, after closing up the café, Anna was walking Teddy along the beach as usual, she had decided to take a walk to Adam's house. It was Friday and Adam was due back late that evening for the weekend. Anna and Adam spoke each evening and relayed each other's day.

She was looking forward to seeing him and had decided to pop over and put some sausage rolls, quiche and other provisions and nibbles in his fridge as he would be getting home late on the Friday evening, tired and probably ravished. Anna let herself into the house with the key Adam had given her and headed up to the kitchen.

As she placed her bag down, she stopped in her tracks. There on the surface was a half drank glass of bubbly, complete with bright red lipstick marks. "Who the hell are you," came from behind her. Anna twirled round to find a dazzling leggy blonde, glammed up to the nines, glaring at her.

Anna was not sure how to react. "I could ask the same of you," she stated meekly, she had been taken by surprise as expecting the house to be empty. Anna felt very underdressed and disheveled against this beauty.

"I am Adam's wife," she stated defiantly, putting her nose in the air as though she was too good to be in Anna's presence. "Are you the cleaner?" She asked.

"No," stated Anna as calmy as she could, now feeling angry. "I am Adam's girlfriend."

To which the blonde let out a laugh. "You! Goodness, he really has lowered his game," she stated as she elegantly walked over to her glass, picking it up and taking a long sip. "Can I help you with anything?" She asked Anna.

"No, thank you," replied Anna. She picked up her bag and headed down the stairs to the exit. She could hear the woman laughing and muttering under her breath as Anna shut the door behind her.

Tears streamed down Anna's face as she headed back to her house with the provisions she had intended to put in Adam's fridge. Once home, she poured herself a large G&T and tried to call Adam; his phone was busy. Anna didn't know what to think, but she was annoyed with herself for allowing the woman to belittle her.

Maybe she was wrong to get involved with Adam, she just did not know what to think. Unbeknown to Anna, Adam had got the surprise of his life too, when he answered his phone. "Hello, Adam." Adam knew exactly who it was and for a few moments was speechless.

"Sarah?" He stated more as a question.

"Well, yes, dear husband," replied Sarah. Adam hung up his phone and turned it off. What the hell was she doing calling him up out of the blue. After her disappearing act more than two years ago, he needed time to think. He knew Sarah and her conniving ways.

He had put up with it as her husband, but she had lost his loyalty the day she left him without a word. He finished up what he was doing and headed for his truck. All he could think of was Anna, he wanted to get home to her. He didn't trust Sarah and was now worried what trouble she might be brewing.

Adam got into his cab and swore outload as he hit down onto his steering wheel with a loud thud before he started up his engine and headed for home.

Anna kept trying Adam and was just getting the unavailable message. Her head was full of what ifs and questions. She doubted herself, Adam and their relationship. Her mind was running wild and nothing would change that until she got an explanation from Adam but with his phone off.

She was thinking the worst. Had he duped her? Had he had enough of her problems? Had he used his work in London as a cover for re-kindling his relationship with his wife? As the evening went on, she became more and more annoyed at Adam. She had had quite a few G&Ts and her head was spinning as she headed to bed.

Adam's head had been spinning all the way home too, but one thing he knew for certain was that he was livid. Adam's life had turned around since Anna had arrived in it, he was the happiest he had been in years and he had no intention of letting his spiteful wife change that.

As he pulled in behind his beach house, he saw the lights on and his heart skipped a beat. Was Anna waiting for him. His heavy heart lifted as he bounded up the stairs, what greeted him sent his heart sinking in the polar opposite direction!

There stood Sarah, dressed like she was about to walk down the red carpet. Her superficial vainness had always been a trait Adam disliked. "What the hell are you doing here?" Adam blasted.

"Lovely to see you too, Adam. Don't I get a hug?" She asked.

"I don't want you anywhere near me, Sarah, get out of my house," he boomed.

"Your house," Sarah added sarcastically. "I think you will find my name is on the deeds too, dear husband!" Adam could not stand to be near to her any longer. He picked up his coat and headed out of the house, he walked along the beach to Anna's house.

It was late and he hadn't arranged to meet up with Anna until the following day; he just hoped she was still awake. As he approached Anna's, his heart sank as he saw her beach house in darkness. He still knocked on the door but got no answer. He sat on her deck looking out to sea, till the chill started to make him shake.

He headed back home with the intention of going straight to bed. On entering the house, he could see that Sarah had made herself comfortable in his room which had been their old room, before Adam redecorated it. Adam took the spare room furthest away, angry and frustrated.

Adam was on the deck the following morning drinking tea, when a scantily clad Sarah walked out onto the deck. Adam ignored her and looked out to sea. "We need to talk," said Sarah.

"Do we," replied Adam. He left her standing on the deck. What he hadn't seen was Anna. She had decided to pop over before she opened the café and had seen them both on the deck, with tears in her eyes she had turned and walked away. Anna opened the café on auto pilot.

Harry and the regulars had noticed and tried to cheer her up, to no avail. Adam arrived just as Anna was closing up. He was completely unaware that Anna and Sarah had met or that she was even aware of Sarah's arrival. Anna greeted him frostily. "Bad day?" He asked. Anna continued with her lock up routine, ignoring him.

Adam was confused, but suspected that Sarah might have something to do with this, he wouldn't put anything past her and she would have known about them due to the media coverage. Adam walked over to Anna, turned her around and lifted her into his arms. "Put me down, Adam."

"Not a chance," stated Adam with a smile. After a few moments of trying not to meet Adam's glaze, she looked into his eyes and melted, letting out a giggle.

"I think you have some explaining to do, young man," said Anna. Adam kissed her on the lips and placed her back on the ground. They sat on the deck with a beer each as Adam told Anna, what had happened. Anna gave her account of the previous day and that she had seen them on the deck this morning.

Adam pulled Anna to him. "I'm so sorry, Anna, the last thing I want in this world is to hurt you in any way. Sarah is selfish and spiteful, she is after something. I'm just not too sure what at this point."

"Why don't you ask her," said Anna, suddenly feeling annoyed and protective of Adam. She was intent on removing the claws Sarah was attempting to lodge into Adam. Adam wasn't too sure if this was such a good idea, but thought that meeting Sarah head on might resolve the matter sooner. He was concerned however as he could see that Anna was angry.

"I think we should ask her together." Adam saw defiance in Anna. The two of them closed up and headed over to Adam's house.

As Adam pulled up to his beach house, he turned off the engine and turned to Anna. "Are you sure about this?"

"Not really," she replied. Anna thought for a few moments, she was tired of other people dictating her life. "Let's do this," she finally announced. Adam led the way, they walked up the stairs to the kitchen.

Sarah was sat at the breakfast bar drinking some bubbly again, stained with the bright red lipstick. She had her laptop open. "Look what the cat dragged in," stated Sarah sarcastically.

"What do you want, Sarah? This is Anna, this is her home too. You lost your right to be here when you walked out with no word more than 2 years ago." Sarah looked speechless for the first time, both of the women watched as Adam crossed the room to his desk and opened the top door, he pulled out his check book and walked over to the breakfast bar.

Anna looked back to Sarah who was glaring at her. "How much?" Adam asked. There was silence. "Listen, Sarah," said Adam. "You hurt me deeply when you left, it tore me apart and it took me a long time to get back on track. Anna is the best thing that has ever happened to me and I won't let anyone come between us, especially you. How much?" He asked again.

Ouch, thought Anna, Adam meant business. Sarah remained silent. Adam estimated the property value and halved it. He wrote out a cheque for this amount and placed it in front of Sarah. "I will be back tomorrow at 4pm, I would hope that by then you will have vacated my house." Adam turned to Anna. "Shall we?" He asked Anna.

She looked into his eyes and smiled. "Yes," she said as she turned to walk out. "I think you said all that is needed," she added as she felt Adam gently place his hand at the base of her spine as a sign of affection and protection. She suspected this was to confirm to Sarah that she had no place in his life, in case he hadn't spelled it out already!

"Do you mind if I stay at your house tonight?" He asked Anna.

"It would be my pleasure." As they drove Anna said, "Very diplomatically handled, brutal but diplomatic."

"To be honest, I didn't expect it to go that well, fingers crossed that she will actually leave. Once she does, I will get the locks changed and speak with my solicitor. I can pass on her telephone number to them and let them deal with her." Both of them felt a new calm come over them. Adam and Anna opened up the café together the next morning.

Adam stayed on for the day to help out. Anna suspected it was to ensure all was well, she was happy to have him close. Throughout the day, Anna could not stop thinking about what Adam had said about his house being her home too, along with stating that she was the best thing that had ever happened to him and that he wouldn't let anyone come between them. Had he said this for Sarah's benefit or had he meant it?

The day whizzed by with lots of smiles and laughter. Harry had of course arrived for lunch, as did Maggie. Adam had been working on the outside of the café and Maggie had stopped before she came in to chat to Adam. "She has left," Maggie informed Adam.

"Pardon," asked Adam.

"Sarah," stated Maggie with a smile. "I never liked her." she added.

Adam laughed. "I might have known you would be in the know."

"Nothing gets past me, Adam, as you know."

"Indeed I do," said Adam. They chatted a while longer before Maggie headed into the café. Maggie was greeted by everyone inside with warmth and smiles. Anna smiled as Maggie moved from table to table chatting to all of the customers.

There was a wonderful atmosphere within her café. She looked up to see Adam smiling down on her tenderly. Anna felt completely blessed.

The weeks flew by and life got back to normal. Anna stayed at Adam's when he was home, and at hers when he worked away. Molly and Em came to stay regularly. They had also been to see their dad. Anna hadn't asked any details, she thought their relationship with their father was best left with them.

Molly would also stay in the holidays and would often help in the café. She enjoyed being by the sea and still gained much joy from the goings on along the beach. Winter was coming and the nights were drawing in. Adam had taken a couple of weeks off and was fitting new shutters to the café.

Anna loved it when Adam was around. She had asked Adam if he had meant what he said in front of Sarah, when they had confronted her. He had taken her hands in his and stated that he meant every word and more. Adam had asked her to move in with him, but Anna had stated that she liked the set up they had for now.

Adam had insisted that she stay at his when there was bad weather. His beach house was built on Pylons and higher than normal to withstand even treacherous storms and surge floods. Anna had agreed; last winter Anna had a few scary moments in her own beach house.

Anna closed up the café that afternoon and Adam came in to share a beer with her by the fire; something of a tradition when Adam was at home. "I've been thinking, Anna…"

"Careful," Anna replied with a smile.

"This café has seen better days and I know you love every inch of it, but one big storm and it could all be lost, I know that Harry is very aware of this too."

"Go on," said Anna now curious.

"Harry has approached me to remodel and raise his beach house as that's at risk also because it such an old building. I know that money is tight for Harry so I was thinking of asking him if I could buy the café as an investment and to enable him to afford a good build standard. What do you think?"

"Wow," said Anna. "I hadn't seen that one coming." Anna thought for a while. Adam got up and got them another cold beer. He sat back down and looked into her eyes. "I do love this café, however I am aware its falling apart, even without a storm. I am not too sure how many winters it will survive. Buildings do not like the sea air, especially this close to the waves."

"Agreed," stated Adam.

Anna added, "I am also worried about Harry. It would destroy him if he couldn't live by the sea. If we had a big storm, I'm quite sure he would be reluctant to leave, for fear he would never get back."

"That's exactly what Harry said to me." Anna thought for a few long moments.

"I think it's a good idea. Harry's safety is what matters most."

"Good, that's sorted then," said Adam.

"I do have one concern though," said Anna.

"What's that?"

"I'm not so sure I will like the new landlord."

"Ha, ha," added Adam as he pulled her close for a kiss.

The following day, Adam headed over to Harry's with the plans for his beach house re-model. Harry wanted the exact same layout, he just wanted it raised and made storm proof. The new beach house would give him this with triple glazed windows and pre-fabricated panels especially designed for seashore living.

Naturally, there would be a new deck, electrics, kitchen and bathroom. The lighting and most of build was integrated into the panel, of which most would be fabricated off site and then slotted onto the steel frame fitted onto the pylons. The beauty of this meant that the actual demolish and erection would be fast.

Harry agreed with all the plans but looked concerned. "I'm not sure I have the budget for all this, Adam."

"I wanted to talk to you about that," said Adam as he explained what he had to Anna the previous evening. The café had been in Harry's family for a long time, so Adam was not sure how Harry would feel about letting it go. Harry thought for a few moments, then put out his hand, the two men shook on it.

"I look upon you and Anna as family. I have been worried about the café and it's upkeep for some time, before Anna arrived. I had to watch the sea slowly take it away bit by bit and it broke my heart. I have loved the buzz Anna has created and I also love my lunches! It will be nice to know that the café will life on for many more years to come," smiled Harry.

The two men chatted on about the plans for Harry's re-model. Adam was pleased on every account. Harry and the café would be storm proofed and safe. Harry had one less worry and he was looking forward to planning and building the café with Anna's input.

It would be a good investment for him and it meant he could work close to home while completing both projects. Harry would speak to the estate agent about the café valuation and instruct solicitors. He thanked Harry again and headed over to tell Anna the good news.

Anna had closed up the café and was taking photos, when Adam walked in. "Good news," said Adam. "We are the new owners of the beach café." Anna jumped into his arms with a squeal. "No rat required this time," laughed Adam as he swung Anna around.

After a moment, Anna said, "You said we?" Adam gently placed her back on the floor.

"It's not up for discussion, the deeds with be in joint names. You built the business, I'll build the structure." Anna smiled and went in for another hug, resting her head against his chest.

"Thank you," she said. She knew there was no point in trying to fight his wishes. On their way home, they picked up a Chinese take-away and spent the evening excitedly talking about the plans for the new café.

Anna had been taking photos of the café the previous day so she could frame and put up a selection in the new café. She had also asked Harry if he had any early ones and she had found a few on the internet. The plan for the café would be slightly larger; cold counters and a better design for ease of customer and staff movement would be incorporated.

The sea would be the main focus with large by-fold window doors which could be folded back on warm days to merge the café and front deck. The deck would also be larger. Anna would keep the same number of covers, as she liked to be able to run the café herself but not be run off her feet.

But from an investment point of view, the covers could be increased, should they decide to lease out or sell the property in the future. Anna also wanted a room added to be used as an art gallery to allow local artist, photographers and other creatives to display and sell their work. It would also allow her customer to enjoy the talents of the local artists and hopefully, provide the artist with some income.

Adam was sure the development plans would be approved as it would benefit the community; the neighbor, Harry, would be unlikely to object and their very own Maggie, would be on the planning committee.

Adam had started work on Harry's house. All the fabrication had been approved and delivery was due in a week's time, so Adam was busy getting the foundations completed. The crane had been and gone, the pylons and steel frame were in place. The electrics were all ready to connect and Adam was busy building the decks and outside area.

Harry had taken a 2 week holiday to visit friends in Cornwall so Adam was keen to have it ready for when he got back. Anna enjoyed having Adam close by. She would often get lost in thought as she watched him work, creating the new home for Harry. She understood why local people would ask him to build for them, she could tell he cared about the work he did and who he did it for.

His physique showed that the work he did needed strength. His shoulders were broad and thick with power, his waist slim, the muscles in his arms were pronounced and he moved around the elevated structure with ease, often hanging off one strut while lifting and fitting another.

The structure came together quickly and the day of the fabrication arrived. the café was not open as it was a Monday, so Anna stood and watched as Adam and the fabricators quickly erected the structure. All of the panels had windows and fittings built in, they were even decorated.

Each panel also had electrics in, which all connected together and then to the main power source. Anna was impressed with how quickly the new house went up. There were four fabricators and Adam, Anna could tell they knew what they were doing and they all worked in unison.

By mid-afternoon, the house was complete. Anna had fetched a cold beer for all of them and they stood on the deck admiring their work and the view. Before long, the fabricators climbed back into their now empty lorry and maneuvered themselves off site. After waving goodbye, Anna and Adam went in to check out Harry's new home.

Anna was totally impressed. All the bathroom and kitchen fittings were complete, the light fittings Harry had chosen were on and even the blinds were integrated into the windows. "Impressive," said Anna. "Aren't you clever," she said moving in for a kiss. "The view even looks bigger," Anna added.

"We opened up the beach windows so Harry had a better view."

"Harry is going to love it," said Anna beaming. Adam was housing Harry's belongings in his garage and the 2 of them would bring them all over tomorrow, ready for Harry's return on Wednesday.

As Anna and Adam were moving Harry's belongings into the new beach house the following day, Maggie arrived with some flowers and provisions for Harry. She had made him a shepherd pie and brought him milk, bread eggs etc., as she knew he would be tired from his journey home.

"Goodness me," exclaimed Maggie as she entered Harry's new home. "You have done it again. This place looks amazing!" Maggie wandered around the new beach house oohing and awing. Once finished, the 3 friends went over to the café for a glass of prosecco to toast the new home.

Anna lit the fire and the 3 of them admired the new vista which was Harry's new beach house. "It's so reassuring to know that Harry will be safe through the storms," said Maggie. Adam and Anna both agreed. They discussed Harry's return the following day. Maggie was planning a buffet and she had a ribbon for Harry to cut. They were all excited to see Harry's reaction to his new home.

Harry arrived mid-afternoon, just as Maggie was closing up the café. Adam had collected him from Norwich station and Anna watched as he got out of Adam's truck. He stood mouth open for a time admiring the new structure in awe of what was before him. Anna could see tears welling up in his eyes.

Adam carried his bags as Anna helped him to the new deck. Maggie was waiting equipped with scissors for the grand opening. "I now pronounce this beach house open," announced Maggie as Harry cut the ribbon. Harry entered and slowly walked around the house looking at and into every part of his new home. Maggie passed the champagne to Adam to open.

As Harry came back from viewing his new bedroom and bathroom, there were tears running down his cheeks. Anna and Maggie both rushed towards him and engulfed him in hugs. All 3 of them were unsure if the tears were happy or sad, they waiting with baited breath for what seemed like an eternity for Harry to speak.

"Well," said Adam, "do you like it?" He asked with trepidation. Harry looked at each of his 3 friends before he spoke.

"Never in my life did I ever think, that a man like me would ever live in such a wonderful home!" All of them now had tears in their eyes, even Adam, as he handed out the champagne.

"We need a toast, Harry, can you do the honors," asked Maggie.

Harry raised his glass. "To my beautiful house and beautiful friendships." The friends all clinked glasses and repeated the toast. Maggie unwrapped the buffet and they all dug in. Harry continued to look in cupboards and at different vistas around his new home, beaming from ear to ear. Adam had lit the log burner earlier and made sure he had a stock of dry wood; he had also built a log storage bench on the deck.

After the 4 friends had finished eating, Anna and Maggie cleared up the buffet and loaded the dishwasher. Harry had not had a dishwasher before and Adam smiled as the two girls tried to explain how to use the machine to a very confused Harry. "I'll pop over tomorrow, Harry, and go over it again," said Anna. The 3 friends hugged and left Harry to get accustomed to his new home.

As Harry sat at his table that evening having finished the shepherd's pie Maggie had made him. He took in his new home and the view of the moon dancing across the sea. He spoke to his wife as he did most days, even though she had died many years ago. "Well, Ada, who'd of thought it, little old us, living in a grand place like this."

Harry had many visitors over the next few weeks, all wanting to wish him well and check out his new home. Anna would smile as she saw him proudly showing off his new home; he had a renewed spring in his step. Adam had designed the new home to be more ergonomic and easy for a man of his age to look after.

The lighting, heating and all the blinds could be controlled by a simple tablet and he could even turn on his TV and beloved radio, the sound system was wired into the house. Harry hadn't even had heating before, other that his log burner, which never quite heated the bathroom or bedroom.

So the new home with underfloor heating in every room made life so much more comfortable for Harry, which he appreciated much more than he could ever express. He had even stopped wearing his slippers so he could feel the warmth beneath his feet, something he found quite astonishing. He didn't even know that underfloor heating existed, and as for the electronic blinds, Harry thought this was on another level.

Anna would always giggle as she would see the blinds go up and down and lights go on and off as he showed off the new features of his home to guests. It warmed Anna's heart to see Harry happy and safe and she knew that Adam hadn't charged him the full rate, that also warmed her heart. She had found a good man in Adam.

Adam was away working in London, to fulfil his commitments after he had finished Harry's place. The plans for the new café and art display space had been submitted. Maggie was looking after getting theses approved and she couldn't see any reason why they wouldn't be approved, but the normal processes had to be followed, especially as they were increasing the footprint of the original café.

Anna was busy in the café as even in the winter, dogs needed walking and the café was a great place to stop off and warm up and also meet up with friends over something delicious. Harry as usual visited for his lunch. Anna was sure the new home had given him a new lease of life; he seemed younger almost and much happier.

He had always been a happy person but he now seemed to stand taller and move more nimbly. Maybe it was the cozy home and mod cons or a combination of that and the pride he gained with his new home. Many passer-by would stop and admire the new beach house. Harry was often on his balcony pottering.

Adam had put in raised beds behind the two storage benches either side of the deck, so Harry could easily sit and plant or tend these. He had put in winter flowering bedding plants which he would tend and dead head. Anna swore she could see him talking to them.

It was late October and cold. Anna was planning to decorate the café for Christmas, her favorite season. Fabrication of the new café couldn't be started until they received the planning approval and she didn't think the build would now go ahead this side of Christmas, so she was keen to make the most of her last Christmas in the old café.

Anna had also been busy making Christmas cakes and puddings to sell in the café, along with Christmas chutneys and anything else she could think of. Anna loved to cook and have a pot of something ticking on the stove. The customers would often put in an order of whatever was cooking, as the smell wafted to entice them and they knew whatever they would buy would be good.

Anna had been talking to her customers about the new café and the hopeful new addition of a display space for local artists. Many of her customers knew of talented local artists and would put the word out.

While closing up one afternoon, a young lady arrived with a reindeer tucked under arm, it was made of driftwood she had found on the beach, carved and fitted together, giving it a smooth elegant and flowing form. Anna squealed with delight. "How amazing!" She had exclaimed clapping her hands together.

The artist, Charlotte, showed Anna her the portfolio of work. There were many different carving from boats to birds, fish shoals, toad stools and many more. They chatted and agreed on terms. A reindeer display of a mother with two younger deer would be perfect for a Christmas scene on the front deck.

The prices of the pieces and the artist's details would be displayed so if any of her customer wanted to purchase similar pieces, they could contact Charlotte. It worked for all. Anna was super excited as she would not be charging for displaying the work of local artists, but she would take a small percentage of the sale price.

As an artist herself, she knew how hard it to could be to find exhibition space and an unsold work is of no use to any artist. She was now certain her new display would work for everyone. It would connect local artists to new customers and give her customer an enriched visit to the café.

Anna was now in full Christmas mode. She loved the fact that having the café meant she could start planning and decorating for Christmas a month or more earlier than she would decorate her home. Charlotte was bringing her reindeer over that afternoon, while Anna closed up. They would be kept in the café overnight and placed on the deck each morning.

Anna and Charlotte would have a dry run this afternoon. Both she and Charlotte had a few ideas and Anna was looking forward to it. She liked Charlotte and it was exactly the sort of thing she wanted for her new exhibition space, introducing new customer to local artists.

Anna had ordered her Christmas trees—one large for the beach and two small, one for the deck and one for inside the café. She had mulled cider warming—a new Christmas addition for her customers, to warm them from the inside for the chilly walk home and the aromas would fill the café with the smell of Christmas, Anna with excitement.

Anna practically skipped through the day. The mulled cider sold well and the café already had a festive atmosphere.

Anna prepped and closed up the café in super quick time. She was excited to see Charlotte and the three reindeer. She had made space for the reindeer on the deck and she had some lights and spray snow to spray on the deck floor, depending on what the two of them decided would work.

Charlotte arrived and Anna went out to greet her and help to carry the reindeer and the other items Charlotte had brought to add to the display. The two of them placed, moved and maneuvered the 3 sculptures around the deck until they found the perfect place which complimented and made the most of the delightful trio.

"Mulled cider?" Anna asked.

"Oh yes, please, that would be lovely," replied Charlotte. The two of them sat on the deck surveying the display with all the other items they had brought to potentially compliment the display. They sat and mused and chatted. Once in a while one of them would try out the other decorations as they discussed and decided what looked best.

Charlotte had brought moss and lichen, the reindeers favorite food and Anna had produced a staple gun from the café, explaining that the café was being rebuilt in the new year so they could staple gun the moss to the deck. The two girls decided on the final mock up and Anna plugged in the lights which would hang along the back of the deck balustrade, framing the deer.

They had decided the 3 should be placed at the back to the left hand side of the café, to the left of the entrance to the café, so anyone entering would pass by the delightful scene. Anna turned on the café's outside lights and took photos to send to Adam. It looked wonderful. The two of them moved the deer into the café and Anna locked up.

Charlotte had left business cards and catalogues of her work and available pieces with prices for Anna's customers to view, both of them were super excited and feeling very festive.

Anna wrote a small article about the new arrivals and offerings in the café for the festive season and sent it off to all the local press with photos of the deer in their café setting. She hoped this would bring customers for her and Charlotte and maybe a new tradition of a festive trip to her little café on the beach, with its festive coat on. She fell into bed excited and exhausted.

Chapter 16

Anna had finished decorating the café and it looked spectacular, if she did say so herself. She had kept to a cream, gold, silver and white theme with traditional wreaths and garlands she had made herself after collecting holly, ivy and some of the Christmas tree trimmings, adorned with the odd bow and bauble.

Both the outside and inside had swathes of garlands, twinkling from every corner. Charlotte had brought some more sculptures including small nativity scenes, decorated Christmas trains and small festive figures, catering for every budget. She had also brought some Christmas tree decorations which Anna displayed on a small white tree she had from last Christmas, which looked delightful.

There was even a small seal pup, complete with a festive Christmas scarf. Charlotte had been so excited to have somewhere to sell her creations. She had got whittling, using all the small off cuts she had never found a use for. Anna had agreed that for anything sold in the shop, she would take a 20% commission on the sale price.

Charlotte was happy, as was Anna. She was delighted to be selling work by a local artist already, especially as the materials had come from the beach. She also had a lot of interest from other artist's and she already had an email list, so she could let them know when the new display space would be opening.

It was mid-December. Charlotte's creations were flying off the shelves and she noticed an increase of children in the café, lost in Christmas wonderment at all the decorations and Charlottes creations dotted all over the cozy café, warm from the log burner and the smell of Christmas within.

Anna had also started making Christmas gingerbread biscuits decorated with brightly colored icing. She had also purchased another bain-marie with 3 pots—1 for mulled cider, mulled wine and hot chocolate, which she decorated with whipped cream and marshmallows, topped with a small red and white cady cane.

Anna loved working in the café at this time of year and she enjoyed being able to sprinkle her own bit of festive magic for her customers to enjoy, but she particularly enjoyed seeing the wonderment in the children's faces. Every day she was thankful for such a wonderful life.

Anna hadn't seen Adam for several weeks. He had been wrapping up all his work before the Christmas break. Adam hadn't told Ann that he was coming home. He wasn't too sure himself, but he had managed it a week before Christmas and had booked to take 2 weeks off.

It was late afternoon when Adam headed to Anna's. He knew that if she wasn't at her house, she would be at the café, further along the beach. As expected, Anna's house was in darkness so Adam headed on. As he turned the corner, he was taken aback by the festive sight. Anna had really outdone herself.

As Adam approached the café, he could see Anna singing along to herself, he suspected Christmas music. Anna was busy decorating another batch of gingerbread biscuits. Adam stood and watched Anna for a while. He had really missed her. He thought she looked angelic inside the twinkling café, his angel.

When Adam finally approached the front of the café, Anna looked up. Within seconds, she was heading around the counter and as Adam opened the door, she jumped into his arms. "This is becoming a habit," laughed Adam.

"Why didn't you tell me you were coming home?" Anna asked.

"I wasn't sure if I would get away today," said Adam. "This place looks amazing. These must be Charlotte's creations," he said as he picked up a rounded snowman from one of the shelves.

"Yes, they are flying out. Mulled cider?" She asked. The 2 of them sat by the fire and chatted. Adam kept spying new elements in the café. Adam announced his 2 week break which made Anna's day. "We can plan Christmas," squealed Anna as she jumped up and planted a long and lingering kiss on his lips.

The 2 of them headed back to Adam's along the beach. The one plan regarding Christmas which was already set in stone was that Maggie would be hosting again. They decided to pop in on her on their way home. Maggie was of course delighted to see them, bustling to get prosecco and nibbles.

Anna and Maggie chatted, mainly about Christmas like two excited school girls. Adam rolled his eyes but smiled all the same. His mother had always been super excited about the

Christmas period and it made being with Anna familiar to the seasons of his past.

Maggie invited them for a take-away the following evening. "I love Chinese and you can't really order for one," she had stated which sealed the deal. "Then we can finalize the Christmas plans."

Adam didn't realize there were more plans to finalize but clearly the two girls did. They bid their goodbyes and headed back to Adam's, Anna had stopped off at hers and picked up a few bits. She already had most of what she needed at Adam's.

Anna headed to the café the next morning. Adam had a few things he needed to sort, having been away working for a few weeks. Adam headed over to the café at closing time to walk Anna back to Maggie's for the take-away. Maggie was ready for her guests with drinks poured and table laid.

They ordered an array of dishes, including crispy chilli beef, sweet and sour prawn balls, chow-mien and crispy squid. Maggie and Anna chatted about Christmas day. Harry was invited as were Anna's girls, and Anna was going to be doing her personalized crackers. Maggie's son was going to his wife's parents for Christmas day this year so it worked out well for all, and Maggie's hospitality could not be faulted.

Anna, Adam and the girls would open their presents at Adam's and would head over around mid-day. The girls were naturally overly excited about the season and both chatted about decorations and the menu. Beef wellington was to be the main event as it was last year. Maggie had hired the same company to cook and serve the Christmas dinner and lay out the evening buffet.

Anna and Adam had decided to head to Norwich on the Monday before Christmas to do some final Christmas shopping. Anna had already bought and wrapped most of her presents. They had also booked a table at the Rushcutters Arms for late afternoon, Anna's favorite Norwich restaurant.

An old coaching house by the river, rumored to be haunted by the disfigured ghostly form of a passenger killed in a head on rail accident in 1874, where 25 souls were killed and the pub was used as a makeshift mortuary. Anna loved a bit of history and Norwich was abundant with it.

The food was always good and there were open fires in the winter. Anna regularly had lunch there with her parents before they passed so it held fond memories for her. The two wandered through the shops, making a special trip to John Lewis, formally Bonds.

Anna's mother didn't visit Norwich, she visited Bonds and Anna remembered spending all day in the store, being sent to find her big sister who always got lost, before lunch of a sausage roll and a Coca-Cola, which was always a treat back then.

Laden with bags, the two of them headed for Adam's truck. It was dark when they pulled up at The Rushcutters Arms and headed into its cozy welcome. The fires were lit and the ceilings were low. It was like a hug in a pub.

The waiter led them to their table which was through the narrow bar and by a window close to the fire overlooking the river. This was Anna's favorite table and she had requested it. It brought back nice memories of years gone by, some with her ex-husband before the love had ebbed out of their marriage.

Adam hadn't been to the Rushcutters before. It had an old style feel which had been brought up to date without losing its old time charm. Adam had to duck under the original beams in the main bar. He also noticed the pub allowed dogs in certain areas and had dog bowls and biscuits.

They decided to have the two starter sharing boards as their main, one included lamb and rosemary koftas, Korean BBQ chicken strips, crispy salt & pepper squid, garlic and coriander flatbreads, houmous, dips and relish. The other was a rosemary and garlic camembert, crudités, red onion chutney and cheese and mustard straws, along with a side of thrice cooked chips; all washed down with a cool pint.

Just what they both fancied after a busy day shopping. The pub's atmosphere was wonderful and very festive; the perfect end to a Christmas shopping trip.

Once home that evening, they both sat on the floor in front of the fire wrapping presents, reminiscing about Christmas' past, they had Christmas songs playing and warming mulled wine. Once finished, Adam sat back on the sofa and watched Anna arrange, re-arrange and then re-arrange again the presents under the tree.

Adam was glad to let Anna take control of what was clearly an important Christmas present placement operation. Adam sipped his drink watching as Anna tinkered with the presents under the tree, amused by her antics. Adam had always wanted children and a family; here he was watching his own families traditions for the first time and he could not be happier.

Christmas Eve arrived and Anna jumped out of bed in excitement. Adam smiled, still amused by Anna's child-like excitement about Christmas. Em and Molly were arriving today and they were all staying at Adam's, as he had 3 bedrooms and was much bigger and more luxurious than Anna's little place.

Anna had decorated Adam's beach house for Christmas. She had also hung four stockings on one of the beams, along with mistletoe. She was doing a Christmas Eve buffet for tea and wanted to get everything done before anyone arrived. She had purchased a couple of platters from M&S which Adam was collecting to ease her workload.

She had ordered some fresh bread which she had added to the list of items she wanted Adam to collect from town, including oysters, crab, mussels, prawns and lobster, all on order from Davies fish shop in Cromer.

Em and Molly arrived at 2. The buffet was due for 5pm. Molly bounded into the house super excited. She was like an over excited Tigger as she hugged and kissed everyone while stealing morsels to eat and wowing at the decorations. The 2 girls settled into their bedrooms.

Anna had laid them out new pajamas and stocked their bathrooms with their favorite toiletries. She had also placed glass jars in their rooms containing their favorite sweets. Although, her girls were all grown up, Anna still liked to treat them when she could. Adam was on drinks duty.

He had taken everyone's order and was busy preparing them while the girls unpacked. Anna had already laid out the buffet items which did not need to be in the fridge and the table was dressed in a festive fashion; everything else was plated and ready to go in the fridge.

Anna collected individual butter dishes and she had used her butter spoon to roll out decorative coils of cold butter, which she added to each dish and dotted around the table.

Teddy was merrily following her every move, thankfully he couldn't reach the table.

The 2 girls came up and they all took to the sofas to start the festive period with a drink, the three girls were having a Prosecco Parfait Cocktail, with prosecco, a touch of gin, raspberry liqueur and topped with fresh raspberries. Adam had gone for an Old Fashioned, a whisky based cocktail. "Goodness," exclaimed Anna. "I'd better not have too many of these or I'll never get the buffet out."

Spirits were high as they chatted excitedly. The girls were eyeing the presents under the tree, wondering which one's were theirs. Teddy was spark-o on the sofa between the two girls. The fire crackled and the festive light on the tree and around the house sparkled as the light of the day faded.

Adam sat back and purveyed the scene. This was the family life he had longed for; it had arrived in an unusual fashion, but he could not be any happier than he was at this moment. Anna caught sight of him, smiling at the scene before him, their eyes met and she mouthed 'I love you'.

Adam smiled and crossed the room to her placing a kiss on her forehead, before he asked, "More drinks anyone?"

Anna laid the rest of the buffet, ready for the arrival of Maggie and Harry. She would unwrap everything once everyone was in and settled.

She had made Marie-rose for the prawns, saffron mayo for the mussels, there were crab and lobster canapes, a sandwich platter from M&S with smoked salmon and cream cheese, ham, cheese and onion, brie and camembert amongst other delicious offerings; Christmas was after all, a time to celebrate.

There was a cheese board with crackers, nuts, crisps and dips, quiche, sausage rolls, potatoes salad, humus, veg sticks, marmalade glazed ham and lots, lots more.

Maggie and Harry arrived, full of festive cheer. Everyone welcomed them and helped with their coats while Adam fixed the drinks. Maggie sat down with the 2 girls. "Right then, tell me all about what you 2 lovelies have been up to." Harry wandered over to where Adam was making the drinks and Anna put the finishing touches to the table.

Soon they were all sat with drinks in hand, toasting to Christmas Eve. Everyone tucked into the buffet; they were so lucky to have such fresh seafood on their doorstep.

Harry dozed in his chair after they had all had their fill of the buffet, periodically chipping into the conversation before falling back into a dose, making Molly giggle who attempted conversations with the napping Harry, much to everyone's amusement of the double Dutch Molly exchanged with Harry.

None of the group wanted to be up too late on Christmas Eve so after a few drinks, Harry and Maggie made their moves to leave. Adam called them a taxi as he didn't want them walking the beach late at night. After they had left, the 2 girls headed for bed. Anna finished up clearing away the buffet while Adam stacked the dishwasher.

Teddy was let out for his final business as Adam and Anna walked onto the beach to pick up any deposits made. Adam put his arm around Anna's shoulder as they looked out to sea. "I love Christmas by the sea," said Anna.

"Me too," agreed Adam. The 2 of them watched the waves for a while.

"Can you hear that," said Anna.

"Hear what?"

"Sleigh bells," stated Anna. Adam kissed Anna on the forehead.

"You really do love Christmas, don't you."

"Yep," was her happy reply. They both listened for a while. Anna could swear she could hear sleigh-bells. "Come on, let's head to bed or Father Christmas won't come." Anna laughed and let herself be led up the steps of the deck taking one last look at the nights sky.

She always thought she could hear sleigh bells on Christmas Eve, a distant memory of her mother opening her bedroom window before bed and convincing her that she could hear sleigh bells many Christmas Eve's before, came into her memory as she wiped away a tear before anyone saw it and headed back into the house.

She would never stop missing her parents, and Christmas was a time to remember all the happy memories of the Christmases in the past.

Christmas morning arrived. Anna was first up. She laid out the breakfast table with pastries, fruit, yogurt and juice. She popped some bacon into the oven along with part baked baguettes. She made herself a cup of tea and went onto the deck to let Teddy onto the beach.

It was early so the beach was deserted apart from the odd regular. Once Teddy had relieved himself and deposits picked up, Anna and Teddy went inside. Anna popped on Christmas music in the background and selected an appropriate Christmas movie on terrestrial TV, which she put on low.

Adam was the next one up. "Merry Christmas, princess," he said as he planted her with a long lingering kiss.

"Merry Christmas," she replied with a warm smile. Adam had the fire going by the time the girls got up. Anna made up the bacon baguettes and placed the in a warmed platter for anyone to help themselves. Molly had already grabbed a chocolate croissant before dive bombing the comfy chair overlooking the beach, expectant of a good display this Christmas morning.

"Bucks fizz anyone?" Anna asked. All accepted, the 4 of them settled on the sofas with breakfast and fizz.

"Can we open the presents now," piped Molly, clapping her hands and jumping up without a response.

"Go on, Molly, you do the honors," said Anna. Molly handed out the presents one by one. There was lots of excitement, thanks and hugs. Teddy received a stocking and a new bed each year, which he proudly rearranged before sitting in it to claim it his. Everyone was very happy with the gifts they received and the next hour was spent pursuing their own and each other's gifts.

Once everyone had showered and changed, they headed for Maggie's. Anna wore a beautiful cashmere wrap and diamond stud earrings which Adam had given her. Molly and Em, both had new tops and handbags and Adam wore a new shirt Anna had given. Teddy sported a Christmas bandana.

There were quite a few families walking on the beach, some with Santa hats or festive attire. Harry was already at Maggie's sat close to the fire when they arrived. He rose as they walked in. Maggie handed everyone a glass of champagne and they toasted. "Merry Christmas." They sat on the sofas chatting merrily about their mornings and the gifts they had received.

The private catering firm had provided a chef and a waiter. The smells coming from the kitchen were tantalizing all. Anna didn't want to disturb the chef but couldn't help herself. She was very interested in what was going on behind the scenes and how private catering worked.

Thankfully, she knew the chef as she regularly visited the café and they had become friends, so she was happy to chat with Anna as she cooked. Most of the dishes had been part of fully cooked in their professional kitchen and were ready to be finished off or reheated. The beef fillet was pre-cooked to perfection, cooled and wrapped in puff pastry, layered with Parma ham, smothered in pate and mushroom duxelles, then chilled ready for cooking. The team had collected any serving dishes they needed a few days before.

Anna left the chef to get on with it and joined the guests in the lounge. The waiter was keeping everyone topped up with drinks, in between helping the chef in the kitchen. Maggie was in her element. She was the lady of the house and she was enjoying every minute of it.

Maggie had laid a beautiful table with gold crackers which Anna had filled. There was a crisp white table cloth, with a silver runner. There were three low bowls with white roses and hydrangeas in, set along the center of the table. Each setting had fine silver cutlery and a napkin rolled inside and plane silver napkin ring simply encrusted with a few tiny crystals.

Each setting had four beautiful crystal glasses again encrusted with the odd tiny crystal, for the red and white wine, water and champaign. There were tiny silver condiment pots dotted around the table, each with a tiny spoon which fitted into the notch in the lid. There were also tiny silver salt and pepper pots and small glass candle filled domes dotted around. It was simple, tasteful and stunning.

Dinner was served. The plates came out with a generous slice of perfectly cooked beef wellington. The waiter went around the table serving the vegetables and all the trimmings to each guest. There were pigs in blankets, roast and mashed potatoes, brussels, red cabbage, Yorkshire puddings and more.

Each guest also had an individual pot of gravy placed beside them. For the first time that day, there was silence. Maggie smiled as she looked around the table at her guests who had become more like a family to her. She felt tears well-up within her eyes until Anna finally broke the silence.

"This is divine, Maggie," said Anna; everyone made umming noises in agreement. Maggie blinked back the tears as the wine was poured, and Maggie raised her for a toast.

"Merry Christmas everyone." The friends all clinked glasses wished each other Merry Christmas.

After the main course, as the waiter cleared the plates, everyone opened their crackers. Maggie received a beautiful clear glass pendant on a long silver chain, encased in delicate silver filigree, containing 6 tiny stars, representing the 6 of the friends around the table, which brought Maggie to tears.

Em received dainty pearl stud earing with 3 tiny cubic zirconia laid into each pearl. "They are beautiful, Mum," she exclaimed. Next was Harry who received a silver key-ring engraved with his initials on one side and words on the other which read 'Friends are like stars, you can't always see them, but they are always there'.

"For your new house keys," stated Anna.

"Thank you," said Harry. "I am so lucky to have such amazing friends," he said as he tried to hold his composure. Molly was next. She received the silver bobble bracelet she had always wanted from Tiffany.

"Thanks, Mum," she said with gusto as she leapt from her seat and gave her mum a bear hug. Em and Harry who were sat either side of Molly had to steady all the glasses she sent wobbling as she jumped up.

Adam was next. Anna had researched his surname and heritage, found his family coat of arms and had a signet ring made for his little finger; it came with a scroll detailing his heritage. Adam leant over and kissed Anna, whispering, "Thank you," in her ear.

"Now for Anna's turn," stated Maggie, as she passed a cracker to Anna. Anna opened it and jumped from her chair; it was the planning consent for the new café, Anna gave Maggie a big hug as her mind filled with excitement and ideas.

"This is amazing, Maggie, thank you so much!"

The waiter brought out the puddings, Christmas pudding and chocolate yule log. He also popped the cork to the champagne as everyone cheered. Everyone's glass was filled with champagne and the six of them clinked glasses and toasted to the festive period again.

The caterers cleared up and left as the 6 friends settled to play the queens speech on catch-up. After a walk on the beach, they all settled for an afternoon of games, drinks and chatter. Maggie and Harry both had gifts for everyone which Molly had spied under the tree and had been tasked with being Santa again and give out the gifts.

The festive celebrating went on late into the evening as their annual tradition was cemented for future years to come.

Chapter 17

Anna was so excited about the new café. She had battled with Adam about contributing to the cost, but he had insisted that it was an investment. Anna was like a child in a sweetshop as she chose the new oven, fittings and fixings.

She would have self-service chilled and heated cabinets with rails in front where customer could place their tray as they chose what they would like to eat and drink, then move along to the counter which would hold lots of goodies they could add to their meal or choose to take away with them.

The café would still open Wednesday to Sunday, from 10 till 2, with the same amount of tables. There was plenty of room for more tables, but for now, keeping the same number of covers meant Anna could run it with ease, while giving her enough time to cook and replenish each day before and after closing.

The design would be simple, rustic but clean, keeping with the theme of the original café. It would be much more spacious, focusing on the view and of course there would be the addition of the gallery space which was already booking up, much to Anna's delight. There would also be a very large central fireplace, open on all 4 sides to add a touch of rustic luxury to the place and warm the guests on chilly days.

The front of the café had by-fold doors which could open the café up, to join with the deck, making for a stunning view, whether inside or out. Part of the deck around the café would be covered for the winter walkers to shelter from the weather and there would be outdoor wood burning stoves, and panels which could be pulled out on rollers from the interior of the buildings shell to shelter outdoor guests during the colder season.

The plans had been finalized and all the interior surfaces and fittings agreed. Anna had gone for a distressed wood effect for all the walls and the lights had a traditional coastal look to them inside and out. Adam would help with the footings and frame and once that was in, he would build the deck. Anna closed up the café that day with the thoughts of the new café in her head.

She looked around her nostalgically. She would be sad to see the café torn down, it was such a big part of her new life. Somewhere she called her own, where she had found herself and grown. The fabricators had started on the café and a date had been agreed to take down the old café and install the new in 2 weeks' time. Anna was not looking forward to that day.

The February snow had started to melt and slush was the name of the game, grey brown sand mixed slush. They had ticked over even in the worst of weathers, with loyal locals wanting to meet up and watch the goings on of the beach from the cozy café. A severe weather warning had been issued with a potential of sea swells.

Anna had already started to move much of the café's contents to Adam's garage, in preparation for closing the café before it was pulled down. Anna opened up as usual, not expecting many guests, if any, but she wanted to savor her last few days in the café.

Anna and Adam had secured the café as best they could at the start of the winter season, but the café was old and may not survive a powerful storm or sea serge. A few local customers came through the door, relieved she was open; partly to shelter from the bad weather, but also to say goodbye to the old café.

Harry also braved the weather for his lunch. Much like Anna, he was going to be sad to see the café go. He knew it had to happen, but he was sad all the same as memories of his family in the old café flooded back. By half past 1, the café was empty. One of the locals had walked Harry back to the safety of his beach house much to Anna's relief.

The weather had picked up and the tide was coming in. Anna loaded what she could into the car. Back in the café, she received a call from Adam. "Where are you?" He said.

"At the café," said Anna, surprised by such a question.

"Anna, leave now, that café is not safe in this sort of weather."

"I'm leaving soon, just finishing up," replied Anna, unconcerned.

Adam was unusually on his way home early. He wasn't happy to leave Anna and the rest of his friends alone during storms like this. He was happy that the beach homes he had built could withstand even the worst storms, but the ocean has its own rules. It's not governed by anything or anyone, apart from the moon, the universe at large and its own unbridled power.

The ocean could never be underestimated and he also knew that his local community would need all the help it could get during bad weather. He was about an hour away when he called Anna. He had told her to drop everything and get back to his, but he suspected she would stay as long as she could. He was right.

Anna closed down all the shutters in the café and went inside to double check she hadn't left anything of importance. The wind was battering the café and she could feel the building move with the power of it, creaking under the strain. When she eventually finished up, she found that locking the café was not easy as the wind had got up so much and she had to battle to get the door shut and stay on her feet.

When she had finally closed and locked the door, she struggled on the short walk to the car. The wind was raging now and the rain was coming down in sheets. Sand was being whirled into her eyes and she had to hold on to any structure available as she tried to make her way to the car.

When Anna finally made it into the car, now rocking in the wind, Anna worried about how the café would fair in the storm. The sky was dark and sea was rough. Anna was about to start the car when she realized she needed to unhook the oven from the gas bottles and lock the gas cylinders closed, not doing this could leave the cylinders open and a spark might cause an explosion.

With Harry next door, she couldn't leave without securing them, but she wasn't looking forward to getting back into and out of the café. After a few moments, she gathered her courage and got out of the car.

Anna had to battle against the wind and rain again to get back to the café door. The gas cylinders were located in a small shed beside the café, which needed to be entered through the café. There was a back door to the shed but Anna had no idea where the key was. Anna could hear the waves unusually close to the café as she entered.

Anna tried to turn on the lights, they flickered but went out. "Shit," she said outload. The shutters had closed off any light in the café. Anna headed towards the kitchen. She knew she had a torch there and she would need it to make sure the cylinders were off. She scrambled around in the draw where she kept the torch and finally located it.

She could hear the water under the café now; this did sometimes happen on high tide, but this was unusual and it had never happened when the sea was this rough. Harry had been watching Anna from his house, growing increasingly worried. He was relieved to see her finally in her car and gave a sigh of relief.

He hadn't seen her get back out of the car. Anna was growing increasingly scared. She could hear the power of the sea around her, the wind and the rain making the sounds even scarier. Anna headed to the shed door as the café floor shifted, like one of the front post had given way.

Anna screamed as she grabbed the counter to steady herself. She could feel tears of fear run down her face. She pictured Harry. What was the point of a safe beach house if the gas was not secured. She scrambled for the shed, she was breathing heavily and shaking.

The whole café felt like it was moving, the now unsecured corner being bounced by the waves. Anna held onto a wooden pillar in the shed as she turned off the gas and fumbled at removing the cooker fixings, before checking and re-checking the gas was off. Once done, she turned to head towards the door when an almighty sound cracked through the café throwing Anna to the floor as another fixing gave way.

She heard glass breaking and the café rocked like a boat on water. She saw the torch rolling around on the floor and made a grab for it. The café felt as though it was still secured at the back, but for how long, Anna had no idea, but she knew she had to get out now.

Anna managed to grab the torch and shone it towards the door, which had gone. The door frame was lifting on the waves and then banging back down against the deck. A large wave must have hit the café as it pushed the front of the café up higher than the back. Anna held onto a post for dear life and braced for the impact as the café crashed back against the deck, just as a large gush of water entered the café.

Anna was frozen holding on for dear life. The tide seemed to lessen and for a moment and the café went still. Anna knew this may be her last chance to make a run for it. She stood up as lights shone into the café and she could see the exit, she ran for the door and launched herself towards the bank at the back of the café.

Adam's truck had provided the light and he was already out of it heading towards where Anna was launching herself. Adam could hear the next wave crashing closer as he grabbed hold of Anna, placing her upright and yanking her by the hand. They both ran for the truck almost blinded from the rain and salty sea spray.

As they got into the truck and closed the doors to the deafening sound outside, the next wave hit, sending the whole café lurching forward into the truck. The back of the café engulfing the front of the trucks bonnet. For a few surreal moments, time seemed to stop and they were in the truck, in the café kitchen.

Anna jolted back to reality as Adam put the truck into reverse as the wave took the café with it on its ebb back into the ocean. Anna watched as the café folded into the waves. Adam put the truck into gear and pulled away at speed.

Harry had shot to the window when he heard the loud bang and saw Anna's car still there. He saw the café front end lifted by the waves as Adam pulled up. He saw everything with baited breath, relieved to see the two of them enter the truck; then gasped as the café seemed to engulf it, before it sailed away and much to Harry's relief, he saw Adam's truck drive off.

Harry stood and watched as the café folded into the waves and disappear into the ocean, it had been like watching a real life action move. Harry uncharacteristically said out loud, "Fuck me," as he fell back into his seat. Before he got up and went to pour himself a very large whiskey.

They arrived at Adam's and battled to the front door, the waves were lapping around the pylons under the house. Once inside the quiet was deafening after the experience Anna had been through. Adam headed up to light the fire as Anna took a shower and put on a warm dressing gown.

As Anna arrived in the kitchen, Adam spun round. The angry look on Adam's face took Anna's breath away. She had never seen that look before. "What the hell were you thinking of, Anna?" Adam boomed, scaring Anna and making her jump back like a frightened child.

"You were lucky to get out of there alive," he shouted again, before turning to take hold of the large glass of whiskey he had poured and swigged it down in one, before pouring another; slamming the bottle back on the counter. Anna started with a stammer, still scared of the angry man in front of her.

"I, I was about to leave…I was in the car…when I realized the gas cylinders were still attached and open. If I had left them…" she tailed off. Adam had his back to her leaning against the kitchen surface, his shoulders taught with anger. Anna had never seen or heard him like this and it terrified her.

A few moments passed and she could see Adam physically relax, probably realizing what Anna had thought, before she got back out of the car. "I'm sorry," said Anna. Adam turned to face her, his features had softened.

"No, I should be saying sorry. I shouldn't have shouted at you. It just scared me," he said, as all the anger disappeared out of him. He realized she had risked her life to prevent any harm coming to anyone else. He walked the few steps across to her, lifting her into his arms and hugging her like a child would hug a rag doll.

Anna felt all the tension leave her. She was safe. Adam placed her back on the floor. "I should imagine you need a stiff drink," he said. Anna nodded, heaving a huge sigh of relief.

As Anna sat by the fire Adam had lit, drinking a large gin and tonic, Adam was on the phone. He was speaking with the local coast guard about the size of the potential swell. He knew at what point it would be dangerous to stay in the house.

He had also checked on Maggie and Harry, telling them to contact him if they wanted to move inland. As Adam put down the phone, the front door slammed open and shut again. Adam and Anna looked at each other, as Molly bounded up the stairs,

"Wow, it's insane out there," she stated as she headed across the lounge and launched herself into the chair overlooking the ocean.

"Molly, what the hell are you doing here?" Anna boomed, it was her turn to be angry.

"I wasn't about to miss out on a ringside seat for the storm of the decade." Anna sighed and shook her head, she knew it was pointless chastising her.

"I wonder where she gets that from, Anna," smiled Adam. The 3 of them sat and watched the angry ocean. The only sounds were from the cracking fire and the crashing waves. The sky periodically lighting up streaks of lightning followed by large bangs of rumbling thunder. It truly was spectacular.

Molly would roar when a large wave would throw water up to crash against the glass doors. "Are you sure this is safe?" Anna asked Adam.

"This place is built with the same construction as an oil rig. It's designed to weather the worst kind of storms. There are also sensors which will set off alarms if the weather threatens our safety," he reassured Anna.

The storm battled against the house for several hours, much to Molly's delight. Adam regularly spoke with the local authorities, Maggie and Harry. He had advised they stay alert until the worst of the storm subsided.

From within the house, it was like it was sailing on the ocean without the movement. The streaks of lightening would light up the sky, revealing the large waves, violently crashing into one another. As the swell began to edge is way back to where it had come from, the 3 of them headed onto the deck.

The sea was still all around them, a sight Adam had never seen before. "It's spectacular!" Molly declared, total enthralled by the evening's entertainment. It was still dark but Adam could tell the beach landscape had changed; only dawn would reveal, just how much.

The 3 of them sat up till dawn watching the storm. They periodically napped on the sofa and Anna made them snacks throughout the night. Adam wanted to stay alert in case he was needed here or elsewhere and he periodically checked in with the coast guard and local police. As dawn arose and the sea had given back some of the beach, the 3 of them wrapped up and took Teddy onto the beach.

Anna was keen to walk as far as the café, also wanting to check on Maggie and Harry, along with her own beach house. Adam had already reassured her that the locals, police and coastguard would vacate any properties which might be in danger. All were used to dealing with storms like this on occasion.

The beach was littered with debris, but also smoother than normal. As they walked, they saw Maggie's house standing proud. Anna looked at Adam. "I had no doubt. If I had, I would have moved her myself," he stated. They passed several with deck damage and the odd one, that was no longer there.

Some had frontal damage and you could see into the living spaces as they turned the beach corner to where Anna's beach house was. Anna gasped; she could see into her living space. The deck and front of the house had gone, the ceiling was hanging into the lounge and no furniture could be seen.

She stopped in her tracks with her hand to her mouth, in shock. Adam put his arm around her shoulders as they stood and looked at the destruction the ocean had dealt to the little beach house. "Looks like you are moving in with Adam for a while," said Molly matter-a-factly.

"Come on," said Adam. "We can come back once it's safe to enter. I'll get it made safe once we get home." The 3 of them continued on along the beach as Harry's place came into view. The lights were on and all looked well. They continued to walked towards it to see if any of the café was left. As they became level with Harry's, the site of the café came into view.

They all stopped and stared. It was like the café had never been there. Anna walked over to the site, she felt a shiver go down her spine as she thought back to the previous evening. Adam was watching her and could see what she was thinking. He walked over to her and gave her a hug.

"The new place will look after you," he stated as he held her close. The 3 of them headed to Harry's to see if he was up.

Harry was indeed up, in fact he hadn't slept either, other than nodding off in his chair on the odd occasion. He was beaming as he opened the door to them. "What a show!" He exclaimed as he ushed them in and gave all three a long hug.

He made a pot of tea, as he briefly chastised Anna, causing Molly some confusion before he relayed what he had seen, word for word. Molly sat mouth open, looking at her mum, in amazement. "Whoa!" Molly stated. "Why did no one tell me!" She said finally.

Molly and Harry shared their experiences with gusto, both whooing and wowing at each other's recollections of events. Anna and Adam sat amused. Clearly, Harry had wanted to share his night of excitement and Molly was probably the best person for the job, lapping up every story like a sponge. They said their goodbyes after an hour or so, intending to look in on Maggie before they all headed to bed.

There were walkers on the beach by now. Anna found it difficult to see people staring into her now broken home. Adam got on the phone and arranged for a friend to come and make it safe and board it up. Anna heard the call and took hold of Adam's hand and squeezed it. "Thank you," she said. Adam hugged her to him and kissed her on the forehead.

Teddy rushed for Maggie's deck, bringing Maggie out to greet them. "I'm so glad to see you all safe," exclaimed Maggie as she hugged them all close. "Nice to see you also, Molly. I have hot chocolate on," she stated as she hugged Molly.

As usual Maggie busied herself and laid out pots of tea and chocolate and pastries. "I stocked up," stated Maggie. "You never know who will arrive during or after a storm," she stated. "What a show," exclaimed Maggie also as she finally sat down.

Again Molly sponged up Maggie's experience with utmost enthusiasm! After the chocolate was finished, the 3 wearily headed back to Adam's for a well earnt sleep. Storms and sea surges were something you had to expect living by the ocean, but it always brough the community together. The 3 of them slept soundly till lunchtime.

Adam was the first up and had made a few calls to see if he could be of use anywhere. Local hotels had taken in those at risk, but there were buildings which needed repairs etc., much like Anna's. He lit the fire and left a note out for Anna before he left.

On waking, Anna took a cup of tea onto the balcony, one thing was for certain, she wouldn't be opening the café that morning. She showered and called Adam, offering food parcels of the items she would have stocked or made for the café that day. A support group had been set up in the town hall, to support anyone affected by the storms.

Anna called them and arranged a drop off later that afternoon. Anna baked and packed up sausage rolls sandwiches and anything else she could think of. She also made a large batch of stew and dumplings and some soup. She took along mobile burners and take-away bowls with lids.

Molly offered to help and the 2 of them loaded up the car and headed to the town hall.

Maggie was already there with an urn of hot chocolate. Anna unloaded and left Molly to set up under Maggie's supervision while she parked the car. Anna had also called the bakery opposite the town hall earlier and she collected bread rolls they had agreed to supply for the soup and stew.

The town hall was a hive of activity with locals offering help and those effected by the storm. The degree of those effected was extreme, some had lost everything while others were without power and hadn't had a hot meal since the day before.

Anna's offerings were greatly appreciated and soon devoured or taken away. She agreed to come back the following day with more supplies. Anna felt such a part of the community now and was glad to help. She and Molly headed home for a more relaxed evening.

Molly and Anna continued to support those affected by the storm, by supplying food via the town hall and Adam continued helping re-building and fixing homes damaged by the storm. After a couple of weeks, their efforts were stood down as homes, supplies and power was restored to most of those affected.

Molly returned home and Adam and Anna took a couple of days off, suddenly feeling exhausted by the effects of the last couple of weeks. They took long walks on the beach, went out for lunch and watched movies cuddled up on the sofa. Adam had a couple of weeks work to do in London before he started on the framework for the café.

Anna spent the time preparing for the café, ordering in everything she needed and stocking the freezers ready for the opening. Adam had installed a large chest freezer in the garage to enable Anna to get ahead. Anna had asked Adam if she could be his builders mate for the construction of the pylons, frame and deck.

She was interested in how these building could withstand the storms and she wanted to be involved in every aspect of the build. Adam had happily agreed on the condition that she also supplied refreshments.

Chapter 18
The New Beach Café

Adam and Anna arrived early at the site of the new café. No clearing was required, the ocean had taken care of that. Adam was marking out the site for the pylons ready for their delivery and the arrival of the pile driver. Once the markings were all in place the 2 of them went over to Harry's for a cuppa while they waited for the kit to arrive.

Harry was naturally pleased to see them. "I'm looking forward to seeing the new café go up," he said excitedly. The kit arrived late morning and the pylons were in by teatime. Anna walked around the footage of the new café, it was much bigger than the original.

"I'm so excited," she enthused to Adam as she took in the new site. Many of the dog walkers had popped buy keen to see the new café go up, as was Anna.

The following day, Adam started on the frame, welding the steels to the pylons, A crane had arrived to lower the heavy steels into place and Anna was redundant so she headed to Harry's, and the 2 of them watched from the warmth of Harry's house, chatting and drinking tea as the frame took shape.

Anna liked watching Adam work. You could see the experience he had in the way he worked and directed the machinery drivers. Sparks would fly as he welded and worked in rivets to secure the café frame from the elements.

Harry found it fascinating knowing that his own house had been made in the same way. By the end of the day, the frame was complete. The electric connection was being laid tomorrow and the fabricators were arriving with the café panels in 2 days' time. The following day, they would start on the decks and steps.

Anna was builder's mate as Adam worked on the deck, which quickly came together. They worked well together deciding on the finer details of things like storage and seating benches along with the placement and size of the steps. They had agreed on the main details on the plan, however it was useful that they could make decisions and improvements as the deck went up.

The deck was deep and wide, running the full length of the café and studio. As Adam finished up, Anna fetched a couple of cold beers from the cool box in the truck and the 2 of them sat on the deck looking out to sea. The smell and look of the new deck gave a glimpse of how the new café was going to look.

"Thank you, Adam," said Anna as she lent in to give him a kiss. Adam smiled down at her and put his arm around her shoulder. Seeing her in the café on the night of the storm had scared him.

He realized just how much he loved her and wanted to do everything in his power to protect her and make sure she was always safe.

The day of the café going up arrived. Anna was beside herself with excitement as she jumped around the house, preparing to leave for the big day. Adam was amused by her excitement. She was like a child about to welcome her first party guests.

Anna had loaded the truck with some of the new café's kit. She was so excited to get started. She had been told to watch from Harry's while the panels were craned in. She knew Adam was just being protective and so she agreed and was happy that she would be able to share the excitement with Harry.

Adam continued on with finishing the deck and balustrades while waiting for the fabricators to arrive, which they did at 10am. Anna and Harry watched as each panel was slotted into place. Anna could barely contain herself as she caught sight on the inner fixings and fittings.

As the roof was fitted and fixed and the crane secured, Anna headed over. The fabricators were still securing and connecting all the panels so Anna didn't venture in, but simply admired the external. As the fabricators finished up, Anna collected cold beers and the sausage rolls she had cooked off the night before, for all involved.

They all stood on the deck looking into the café which had its bifold doors concertinaed back. It looked amazing. Anna and Adam congratulated the team, who swiftly finished their beers and headed off.

Anna walked into the café as Adam closed up the glass doors to shut out the cold. "Wow," was all Anna could get out as she spun around slowly taking it all in. The counters and serving space were all fitted and there were spaces, manufactured milometer, perfect to have the chilled and heated cabinets slot in.

Anna jumped into Adams arms. "Thank you so, so much. It's perfect." Adam smiled and kissed her on the nose. Anna wandered into the gallery space as Adam followed her. "Wow," she said again. It was clean and bright, a blank canvas ready for all the artworks to be displayed.

Anna saw Harry looking through his window and she beckoned him over. He was on his way almost immediately. As he entered Anna and Adam both saw his eyes well up. The café had been a big part of his family. Just at that moment there was a tap on the door. Maggie had arrived with Champagne and glasses.

"My! What a wonderful place," she exclaimed.

Adam cracked open the champagne and the 4 friends toasted to the new café, with Adam adding, "Let's hope nobody sails in her!" Causing a ripple of laughter from Maggie and Harry. Anna looked at Adam and rolled her eyes smiling.

Anna sent out emails that evening to the artists letting them know that the café was built and would be opening the following week, informing those booked in that they could install their artworks ready for the opening. The cabinets and oven were being delivered and hooked up the following day and Anna was busy in the café getting it ready for the launch.

Adam was helping delivering table and chairs, along with all the kit being stored in his garage. Adam stocked and lit the fire and filled the wood store. The café looked amazing, so bright and clean but still retaining the old beach café look, with bleached wood effect walls and floor. Adam stood watching the fire flicker as Anna came up and put her arms around Adam's waist and rested the side of her head against his back while she looked out to sea.

Adam turned around and place a kiss on her lips. "I love you, Anna."

Anna smiled up at him. "I love you too, more than words," replied Anna. The 2 of them stood together for quite some time enjoying the moment and the shared love they had unexpectedly found together.

Anna baked and baked in preparation for the opening. Signs had been up announcing the date and Harry had wheeled out his BBQ roaster so that they could celebrate the opening with a hog roast. Anna had ordered a whole hog which they would light early on the morning of the opening. That way if there wasn't room in the café, anyone passing could help celebrate the opening with a hog roll.

Adam, Maggie, Harry and Molly would all help on opening day. Harry would man the gallery; Adam would man the hog roast and Molly would help with the outside serving area and Maggie would help inside. Anna could barely sleep the night before the opening.

Adam and Anna were up and out by 5am to light the hog roast, before returning home to shower and get ready. They were back at the café by 8am.

Adam lit the fires inside and out. Thankfully, the weather was kind and no rain was expected. They had permission to build and light a fire pit in the sand and Adam was busy loading the bales of hay he had delivered in a circle around the fire. Molly was adding blankets to each bail.

The chiller cabinets were all full and Maggie was loading the hot cabinets. By 10am, they were ready and the café opened. The local press had done a feature on the demise and re-opening of the café and even the local radio had interviewed Anna so they expected a crowd.

Locals were already sat chatting on the bails when the café opened, and it soon filled up as did the outside seating. By lunchtime, there was a party vibe surrounding the café and one of the local buskers arrived with her band and started playing around the fire.

At 2pm, when the café officially closed, the customers slowly dispersed and Adam re-stocked the firepit. All those who were involved with or helped with the café had been invited to stay on for drinks and food.

Everyone that had helped that day had worked hard to feed and water all their guests, now it was their turn and they were all famished. First of all they all took a breather with a drink around the fire, discussing the goings on of the day, proud of their achievements. Adam hugged Anna to him, "Well done you," he whispered.

Anna stood up. "I'd like to thank you all for all your help, along with the love and support you have given to me and my family. Cheers to you all and the brand new Beach Café." Everyone raised their glasses and toasted to the café. Anna left them chatting as she put together a buffet on the café counter.

After everyone had dug in and filled their bellies, they all sat again round the fire pit with drinks refilled the friends chatted and warmed by the fire well into the evening. Anna had closed down the café and stacked the left over hog roast in the fridge.

She sat down and heaved a sigh of relief as she leant against Adam and promptly fell asleep. Adam woke Anna as the last guests left and they headed home, both exhausted.

Life settled and the weeks turned into months. Adam cut ties with his contracts in London and decided to focus his time on building and rebuilding local beach homes, which could withstand the onslaught of the ocean and its changes. With Maggie, they lobbied for grants to help locals to future proof their beach homes and to install sea defenses which would reduce beach erosion and the impact of future storms.

Adam bought the freehold of Anna's old beach house plot and agreed within the price, to re-build and future proof the beach home of the couple who had initially rented the property to Anna, which had also been affected by the storm.

Adam, with Maggie's help, negotiated with the council to increase the footings of the original beach house Anna had rented, with outlined planning permission to build a new home for himself and Anna to live in together. Anna had many ideas, as did Molly.

Work progressed on the new beach house. Adam had again designed the building to have the bedrooms on the first floor and the lounge and kitchen above, with a large balcony. The whole building was raised on pylons as before to protect it from future storms.

Anna had at first battled with Adam about not contributing to the build cost, and eventually, conceded when Adam insisted that any funds she had, should be put into savings for the girls as their farther would not be providing for them anytime soon. Anna agreed with the realization that Adam had become her rock and intended to be there for her girls too.

The new beach house would have 4 bedrooms; one for them with an en suite bathroom and one each for the girls, with a spare for guests. The beach café continued to be a haven for beach walkers as well as a destination for anyone who knew about the café, when they visited the local area.

The gallery space was a huge success. Regular sales were made and many of Anna's customer would spend time in the gallery enjoying the space and admiring the artworks on show. Anna loved her new café, as did the locals. She had even taken a few wedding and party bookings.

When Anna closed up, she would often linger in the café and gallery, enjoying the serenity of the building and its views.

The new beach house went up mid-summer, after all the plans were signed off and the panels fabricated. Anna and Adam had been jointly involved with the design and look of the new house, which included a much larger kitchen so Anna could work from home or the café.

Anna was beside herself with excitement as the process started with the marking out, pylons, frame and then the decking went up. On the day of the fabricated panels going up, she could hardly contain herself. Adam laughed as she bounced around the house.

As they arrived on site early, Anna was ushered behind the safety barriers Adam had put in place. This was a much bigger feat than the café or Harry's house and it had to all be done in one day. The crane and panels arrived together. By which time, a crowd had started to gather behind the barriers to watch the goings on.

Adam had a reputation for building beautiful beach houses along this coast which could withstand any storm, so there was a lot of interest. Many setting up deckchairs as it was a beautiful and very sunny day.

Anna stayed out of Adam's way. She knew he had a big day on his hands and she didn't want to add to it. Maggie arrived at lunchtime with a team of helpers who erected a gazebo with seating and set up a makeshift pantry with cold drinks and food. Anna looked at her in disbelief.

"He will need food and refreshments when he finishes," stated Maggie. Anna let Maggie carry on in her usual flamboyant way. Maybe this day did need some flamboyance, after all, Adam was building their forever family home and it should end with a celebration. Maggie had known Adam much longer than she had so she was happy to go with it.

Adam smiled as he saw Maggie setting up. She had done the same for her own house build and although, he thought it was over the top, he had appreciated and enjoyed the evenings celebration and a place to retreat to from onlookers after a similar hard build. He saw Anna looking in his direction and gave her a wink and a smile, seeing the concern on her face.

Anna took that as a green light and started helping Maggie prepare the area. 3 side panels were put up to keep the gazebo cool and provide some privacy; only the view towards the beach house was left open and the back panel had a window in it.

Maggie and Anna sat down with a cool glass of prosecco in the now fully erected gazebo, complete with coolers, chairs and table. It was like a cabana you would see beside a swimming pool in Florida. Anna had to admit that it did make for a more comfortable day and did feel more private amidst the growing onlookers.

Adam walked over mid-afternoon for a very speedy pit stop and took on some cool water, ate and refreshed himself with the cool damp towels Maggie had also brought along, before he headed back to the build. Anna was mesmerized, she had seen Adam work before, but never this hard and with such direction.

He was in complete control of the whole project, foreseeing issues and directing the workforce who clearly held him with great regard. By 7pm, the last of the contractors had left and the house was up. Anna and Maggie had stayed where they were for fear of interrupting what was clearly an intense day.

As the last of the contractors pulled away, Adam headed towards them. He was dirty, disheveled and clearly exhausted but beaming as he walked down the beach towards them. Anna jumped up and grabbed him a cold bottle out of one of the coolers. Adam kissed her on the top of her head after accepting the cool beer and slumped into the chair which looked back onto the house he had just built.

There was a small ripple of applause from the few onlookers that remained on the beach and Adam raised his bottle wearily in thanks. Anna moved behind Adam and wrapped her arms around his neck, resting her chin on her arm, seeing the view he saw of their new home. "I built your palace, princess."

Anna kissed his dusty, salty cheek. Within moments, he was asleep.

Anna sat back down in her chair after fixing her and Maggie another drink. She figured Adam needed a power nap. The two ladies took in the new vista. Anna would wait for Adam to wake before she took a look inside their new home. The two of them clinked glasses and enjoyed the evening warmth and the sound of the waves against the shore as they admired the newly erected home while the builder took a well-earned nap.

Maggie made up the make-shift buffet she had planned for, knowing how exhausted Adam would be, whilst also knowing that he would want to show Anna around the new home he had built for them. Once assembled and still covered, she sat back down with Anna and waited for Adam to stir, they didn't have to wait long.

Adam had a 40 minute nap and awoke with a start, clearly still in building mode. "You finished it," said Anna, laughing as she got up and went over to plant kiss on his salty lips. Adam smiled up at her, stretched and yawned.

"I am starving," he stated. Maggie was already uncovering the buffet as Adam turned to see what the commotion was. "You star," announced Adam as he rose to his feet and started to load a plate.

Maggie had made sure there was plenty of protein along with the usual nibbles with chicken drumsticks, scotch eggs, cold meats and an M&S sandwich platter which included smoked salmon and cream cheese, ham, chicken and bacon and lots more. Adam practically breathed in his plate before going back for more. Anna handed him a cold beer before she and Maggie sat down with their food.

Once everyone was finished, Maggie announced that the she would help the team to break down the picnic. "You too go and explore your new home. Once the boys have packed and loaded up their van and the beach is clear, I expect a guided tour," she stated.

Adam and Anna grabbed a fresh beer each and headed slowly towards their new home, wanting to take in every inch as they approached the new vista on the beach. "Wow," said Anna as she stood at the bottom of the deck. Adam took Anna by surprise, as he lifted her into his arms.

Maggie looked up as she heard the squeal of laughter Anna had let out and smiled as she saw Adam carry her up the stairs and over the threshold of their new home. Adam placed Anna back on the ground in what was the new downstairs entrance space—a sort of luxury boot room, with lots of paneling and storage for coats and shoes and somewhere to sit while you kicked off your beach boots.

It was a large room which was open plan but has specific zones, the coat and boot area, a kitchen area with a fridge sink and glasswasher for fixing drinks and nibbles. There were shelves which were underlit which would act as a bar area for spirits, mixes and glasses to sit. Anna could not wait to get this area set up.

She could imagine just how it would look when fully stocked. The third area had comfy seating. It wasn't large, but just big enough to escape to, should the weather on the large first deck take a turn for the worst. "It's amazing, Adam." Anna has seen all the plans but noting had prepared her for the real thing.

"Come on," said Adam. "Let's see the rest of the house." The two of them visited each bedroom in turn before they entered the master. As before Anna was in ore and in the master bathroom, she jumped into Adam's arms and placed a large kiss on his lips.

"I never dreamed I would ever have such a large bathroom," she said. From the bedroom, you walked into a dressing room which had his and her wardrobes, a dressing table and floor to ceiling mirrors. It was impressive! This lead into a large bathroom with his and her sinks, large bath and a separate double shower. "I could live in here," stated Anna as she whirled around opening doors and testing taps and lights.

Eventually, Adam managed to drag Anna up to the first floor, which was impressively enormous. "Wow," said Anna again and she visited the kitchen first. She could imagine working in such a wonderful space. As she looked up she could imagine all the furniture spread out in front of her as she cooked and then out to the second deck and beyond that, out to sea.

Adam leant against a post as he watched her take in her new home. Seeing the delight and wonderment in her eyes filled his heart with joy and he felt himself well up. "Come on," he said, "let's go out onto the deck. I am sure Maggie is itching to come in, we can give her the nod." Anna skipped after Adam.

As they went onto the deck Adam saw the lads load the last of the beach picnic into their van. Maggie was looking up at them in anticipation and Adam beckoned her over. Maggie was immediately on her way, she didn't need any further encouragement. Adam went down to meet her as Anna took in the new upper deck and views.

It had large bifold glass doors and a large triangle of glass above which gave the upper floor maximum light. The new deck was large with a thick glass balustrade. Anna looked out to sea lost in a bliss of security and excitement. Could this really be her home? She turned around to look back into the beach house.

It looked familiar with all the fittings she and Adam had chosen and she could imagine the wonderful memories they would create in this beautiful home. Adam appeared at the top of stairs followed by Maggie who was flamboyantly cooing over the new house. Anna walked in to greet her smiling. "Oh,

Anna, it's exquisite," she stated giving Anna a big hug. The 3 friends wandered around the space taking in every inch.

After a while, Maggie bid her goodbyes and Anna and Adam wandered out onto the upstairs deck looking back inside. "Well, do you like it?" Adam asked.

Anna turned to him. She still could not quite take in how her life had changed. "If I had dreamt my dream home, it would not have been as good as this," she replied. Adam wrapped his arms around her as they looked out to sea.

Over the next few weeks, they moved in all their furniture. The old beach house would be let out and so needed to be emptied also. Within a few weeks, they had settled in. Em and Molly had been to visit while the house was still a bit of a shell, so Anna had organized a roast for the official family get together once they were settled in.

On the day of the official roast, Anna was busy in her new kitchen as the girls arrived. Comfy seating had been placed in-front of the window to enjoy the views. As the girls arrived, Molly took her place in the window as she scanned the beach for any activity, strangely without her usual leaps.

Anna put it down to it being a new place. The girls loved the new place and made claim on their desired bedrooms. Molly particularly fond of the boot room bar. "This is like a party pad, Mum," she had said. They all sat on the upstairs balcony with a drink, enjoying the view as they waited for the dinner to cook.

After dinner when they were all sat on the sofa, Anna noticed that Molly didn't seem herself. "Are you ok, Mols?" She asked. Molly stood up and walked over to the seats looking out to sea, Anna followed her.

"I'm pregnant, Mum," she said before she burst into tears. Anna engulfed her in a hug, not sure what to say. Em stayed where she was with her eyes welling up with concern for her sister, she already knew. A few moments passed before Anna sat back with Molly's hands in hers.

"All will be well, Mols. We are all here to support you." There was a pause of silence for a few moments before a loud wiring noise was heard coming from the kitchen which made everyone look up and back towards the kitchen. Adam turned to see all three girls looking at him as he turned to face them with big blender jug in hand filled with a garish purple colored fluid.

He stopped and froze unsure what to do or how to act in such a situations. Anna saw his panic. "What on earth are you doing, Adam?" She said with a smile.

"A smoothie for Molly. I put lots of healthy stuff in it," he said as he raised the jug in the air with an impish smile. This made everyone laugh, even Molly. It was the only think he could think of to do to try and help in such circumstances, he'd never had to deal with anything like this before.

Molly, Em and Anna talked long into the evening. Adam spoke very little other than to give Molly his full support in whatever choices she made. Molly was adamant she wanted to keep the baby. She knew who the father was but didn't actually know him as it was a one night stand at a summer festival.

She had finished her studies and had intended to take a year out to travel. That wouldn't be possible now and she would have to take some time out for this new reason. "We will all support you in every way we can, Mols," said Anna. Everyone gave Molly their full support.

Adam periodically laid drinks and healthy snacks out in front of the 3 of them. The atmosphere was finally lightened when Molly teased Adam, "I think you can give it a rest with the healthy snacks, Grandad." This made everyone laugh and cemented what would be the next chapter in this new families life.

Chapter 19

Over the course of the next few weeks, a plan was hatched. Molly would move in with Anna and Adam for the time being and she would help in the gallery space when able. The gallery was becoming increasingly busy with visitors and Anna didn't have the time to be drawn away from the demands of the café.

Molly had studied Art at university, so she was perfect for the job. She could curate the gallery and work on her own artworks. Anna knew her customer would love to see a real artist at work and hopefully, Molly could develop her own career also.

It all seemed like it was meant to be. Everyone was becoming increasingly excited about the arrival of the new baby. Strangely, Adam seemed the most excited. He had surprised the girls one day when they came home to find that Adam had decorated and furnished the fourth bedroom as a nursery.

It was cream and white with accents of color from the accessories. He had even hung pictures of cute bunnies around the room and there was a large giraffe cuddly toy stood in one corner of the room. Molly was overjoyed and gave Adam a massive bear hug. Anna was surprised.

"I didn't realize you had such a talent for nest feathering," she teased. Adam took it all in his stride. He hadn't said anything but this was the next best thing to being a father himself and he was bursting with excitement at the thought of being a grandad. The child's real grandads were not around and unlikely to be for the child's formative years, and therefore, he was more than happy to fill that role.

Adam's reputation for building spectacular beachside homes had grown further with the last few builds and he had been offered a consultancy for building multimillion pound homes by a firm based on the south coast of the England. It was part time, paid well and much of the work could be done from home.

When he did have to travel, he could pick and choose when and would often take Anna and make a short break out of it. Adam wanted to be there for Anna and Molly as much as possible so he didn't want to commit to any projects himself, so it worked well for him. He also didn't to miss a single moment of his grandchild's arrival and planned some time off for the actual due date.

He had negotiated his contract so that he could increase or decrease his commitments as and when needed. The firm had many contractors who could fill for him. Though he knew the firm liked his work above that of the other contactors so he was able to benefit from this and plan his own schedule.

The family had gathered for a roast as Molly had been for her second scan and was going to reveal the child's sex at the gathering. There was an excitement in the air and once everyone had eaten and cleared, they all sat down on the sofas. "Come on then, Mols, put us out of our misery," said Emily.

Molly stood up. She was now clearly showing. She put her hand to her tummy and announced, "It's a baby!" Anna rolled her eyes and Adam laughed. "Ok, it's a...girl." Anna and Adam jumped out of their seats and went over to hug Molly before hugging each other.

Excited chatter about what the new little girl would be like and what plans they all had ensued. Adam disappeared downstairs before arriving back up with a baby cake of pink and white baby essentials, all tied up in a pink and white striped blanket and spotted ribbon and bow, with a cream and white bunny sat on top.

He handed it to Molly before placing a kiss on her head. The 3 girls cooed at the cute and tiny items as Molly opened up the baby cake. "I can't believe how small it's going to be," said Em.

"I sincerely hope it is," stated Molly, which made the girls giggle.

Adam looked towards Em's fiancé and stated, "I'm going to be outnumbered in a house full of females, you and me need to stick together!" He said as he clinked glasses.

"She will have you wrapped round her little finger in no time, and you know it," said Anna.

Adam nodded in agreement, knowing she was right. "Just like you and the girls do," he stated with a smile.

"You are a dark horse," Anna said to Adam later regarding the gifts.

"I bought one of each, a blue and a pink. The shop said I could return whichever wasn't needed. I had hoped we might need both if it was twins," smiled Adam.

"I think you are more excited about this baby than anyone else." Adam smiled and took Anna's hands into his and looked into her eyes. Anna swore she could see tears welling up.

"I always wanted to be a dad and have children. I thought that ship had sailed and I had resigned myself to that. This is closer than I ever expected to get, I have a family that I love and there is now a new baby on the way, I am more excited than you could ever imagine," he said.

With that, Anna welled up too and they hugged, both filled with the unexpected love and the new family which that love had created.

The pregnancy progressed without complications and as the last few weeks took its toll on Molly, she experienced all that many heavily pregnant women experience. "I can't even put my socks on and wearing pants cuts off the blood supply to my legs," mused Molly over breakfast one morning.

Anna smiled remembering her experience of late pregnancy. "If I sat on the beach, passers-by would think I'd been washed up and try to wush me back into sea," she went on.

"I know it feels like your pregnancy is never ending but the baby will soon come," reassured Anna. Adam simply continued on with his breakfast. He enjoyed experiencing all that pregnancy brought while trying to support Molly in every way he could.

As the due date came and went, everyone was on tender hooks expecting the arrival at any time. A plan had been put in place for the café and Maggie would step in with Harry's help at short notice if needed. Adam had also put an agreement in place so that he could take a few weeks out at short notice and he made sure that any work he did could easily be picked up by one of his colleagues.

Anna was busy in the café when her phone rang. It was Molly and all she managed to get out was that her waters had broken before Molly went into a contraction and was unable to speak. Harry was already by her side, having looked up when he heard a sheet pan hit the floor with a clang and saw a spatula fly across the café and hit a wall when Anna saw a call from Molly come up.

"Go, go, go!" Harry said, which Anna did, racing across the beach as fast as her legs could carry her. While running, she called Adam who was in town. Between heavy breaths, Anna got out, "Molly's in labor." Like Anna, Adam dropped what he was doing and charged towards his truck.

Anna raced into the house first. She could hear that Molly was upstairs. Anna found her on the floor in front of the window looking out the beach. Adam raced up behind her. Anna was calling an ambulance as he arrived. "Get clean towels, then warm water," Anna directed Adam did as requested.

He then fetched pillows and a quilt to help make Molly as comfortable as possible. "What can I do?" Adam asked.

"Not a lot, the baby's coming now," with that Molly let out an enormous scream.

"Can you support Molly from behind," directed Anna. Adam sat behind Molly on the floor, his legs either side of her enabling her to lean back on him. She immediately grabbed both of Adam's hands in a vice like grip, causing Adam to wince as she dug her nails into his flesh, surprising Adam with her strength.

Anna didn't know much about delivering babies other than her own experience. She'd had her children at home and remembered the midwife telling her that if she happened to have the baby alone, to wipe its face clean with a towel, and the baby was not breathing, repeat more vigorously and check the airway, repeating this to get the baby breathing.

Once all was well with baby, wait for the ambulance to deal with the cord, etc. Molly let out another scream. "I can't do this, Mum," she growled.

"You can do this, Molly, trust your body."

"I want to push," she screamed. Anna could see the top of the baby's head. There was no going back now, so Anna told her to push with the next contraction. Anna looked up at Adam who had gone white.

"Stay with me, Adam," she said as she tapped his leg, just as Molly let out another scream. "Push, Mols, push down hard towards your bum," said Anna. Molly let out a howl like scream which seemed to come from the pit of her chest.

Adam braced as his hands took another crushing. After what seemed like an age, Anna announced, "The head's out," as she beamed up to Molly and Adam, Anna knew to check that the cord was not around the baby's neck which thankfully it was not. "You need to get the shoulders out with the next contraction, so another big push when it comes," Anna directed and with that the next contraction came.

Again, Molly let out the unearthly growl as she pushed down. Suddenly, Adam felt the vice like grip stop as the baby plopped out. Molly heaved with relief as Anna wiped the baby's face and it let out its first cry. Anna placed the baby on Molly's chest asking her to put the baby to her skin, before Anna covered the baby and Molly with a large towel.

Adam propped her up with pillows as he slowly made his way onto his feet, cramped from sitting for so long in one position on the floor.

As Adam stood up, he heard the ambulance siren and rushed down to meet them and guided them to where Mum and baby were. After the crew had dealt with the cord, etc., they checked the vitals of mother and baby before they helped Molly over to the sofa.

All seemed well. The ambulance crew spoke with Anna and Adam to confirm that all seemed well and from that they saw, there was no need for a hospital visit, but to call if there were any changes with mother and baby. They stated that the birth would be reported and that a midwife should visit within the next day or two. They said to call their GP if they did not hear anything and with that they bid their goodbyes.

Anna was busy with Molly and the baby. Adam went to the fridge to retrieve the champagne he had put in there ready for this very moment. He poured three glasses and took two over to Anna and Molly. "Shall we wet the baby's head," he said.

"Too right!" Molly said, "that flipping hurt." Which made Adam laugh. They all clinked glasses.

"Would you like a hold, Adam?" Molly said. Anna had already had a cuddle.

"I would love too," he beamed as he put his champagne down. Adam gingerly took the baby in his arms. He'd never held a new-born before. "She's so tiny," he said as he looked down at the tiny bundle who was asleep now, having had her first feed with a little help from Anna. At that very moment, Adam could not have been any happier.

Adam doted on his new grandchild. His heart melted as he looked upon her and he was looking forward to being a part of every tiny development in her life. He had already changed a nappy. Molly and Anna smiled as they watched Adam cooing and rocking the new-born. He was totally smitten already.

Anna called Emily to give her the good news and Adam called Maggie and Harry. All were ecstatic and were going to visit the next day. Molly's first night went well. She was breastfeeding for the first few days to give the baby the colostrum, which is full of lots of goodness and antibodies.

Molly was adamant she wanted to bottle feed as soon as possible. The baby had woken to feed several times in the night and Molly was tired when she finally got up at 5am, but the baby seemed content so she was happy with how the first night had gone. Anna arrived up in the kitchen at 6, excited to see the new baby.

Molly went for a shower while Anna kept an eye on the baby who was now sleeping soundly in her Moses basket. Adam arrived a short time later, also excited to see the baby. Molly arrived upstairs and smiled as she saw her mum and Adam both cooing over the baby.

Adam looked up to see Molly and smiled. "I'll sort us some breakfast," he said as he moved towards the kitchen.

After making them all a cup of tea, he started on a Full English along with pastries, yogurt and fruit. He figured a leisurely breakfast would give them all a good start to the day. Adam laid the table and added the juice, fruit and pastries along with jams, butters and a large pot of tea, in between tending to the now cooking breakfast.

He placed the eggs, bacon, sausage, tomatoes, mushrooms and hash browns on a large warmed central platter, adding a bowl of baked beans and a rack of toast. "Breakfast is served, ladies," he announced as Anna and Molly took their focus off the baby. Having been so engrossed with feeding and tending to the baby, they hadn't even noticed what Adam had been up to.

"Wow!" They both exclaimed in unison.

"You read my mind, Adam," said Molly, as she eagerly sat down and grabbed a croissant before she tore off a chunk to munch on as she loaded her plate with the delicious offerings.

"Any thoughts on her name yet?" Anna asked.

"I think I shall call her Tiffany, Tiff for short," she said with a big smile on her face. Adam and Anna both rolled the name through their minds.

"Tiffany," mused Anna. "I like it," said Anna.

"Me too," agreed Adam.

"Tiffany Rose," stated Molly with a nod. Anna and Adam smiled at each other. Anna raised her orange juice.

"Hold that thought," said Adam as he jumped up and grabbed the champagne from the fridge and topped everyone's orange juice up with it, making it into a bucks fizz.

"To Tiffany Rose," proposed Anna, as they all clinked glasses.

Adam cleared up after breakfast. As much as he wanted to spend time with the baby, he knew Anna would be more use to Molly and the baby. Once cleared, he went over to sit with the girls. "Would you like a cuddle?" Molly asked. Adam didn't need to be asked twice, beaming as he looked down on the little bundle.

"Hello, Tiff, how are you today?" The three of them chatted merrily on the sofas when Emily arrived.

"It's Auntie Em's," said Molly. Adam reluctantly handed the baby over to the now cooing Emily.

"She is so gorgeous and tiny. Hello, little lady," she said. Moments later Maggie and Harry arrived. Of course Maggie had brought champagne and macarons, and a rather large cuddly pink flamingo. Everyone gathered round the new baby.

"It's so wonderful to have a new baby on the scene," said Maggie. The champagne was poured and the baby was passed round. Everyone enjoyed the bubble that a new-born creates and the day passed in the blink of an eye.

As evening came, Adam blew up the baby bath he had purchased on the recommendation of a friend, especially for bathing a new-born. Adam filled and tested the water with his elbow as directed by Anna. Anna helped Molly as she gingerly gave Tiffany her first bath, as Adam watched tentatively, noting what was required at every step, keen to help out in the future and to make sure he would get it right.

It was a memory that would last a lifetime as the new-born splashed her legs in the warm water while the fire crackled in the background. Adam watched on as the baby was dried, talked and dressed in a Babygro, a garment which looked highly complex to Adam.

He breathed in the smells that a new baby brought and took in the smiles on the faces of the new mother and grandmother as they spoke softly and tended to the new arrival with great care. Tiffany was passed to Adam to cuddle while Maggie and Anna cleared up. Adam would never forget that smell or the warm softness of a freshly bathed new-born.

The next few weeks and months flew by as the baby fitted into the new routines. Molly did feed the baby herself for the first few days and found it uncomfortable, so changed over to bottle feed which Tiffany took to easily. It also meant that Anna and Adam could help feed her. After a few weeks,

Molly started work back at the gallery, while Adam looked after Tiffany.

Adam loved his alone time with the baby, talking to her and trying to make her laugh with silly noises. He also walked along the beach with her in a baby carrier strapped to his front, often visiting Maggie and stopping off in the café. It would take some time to get down the beach as all the locals wanted to meet the new arrival.

That evening over dinner, Anna asked Molly if she intended Christening Tiffany. "I think I will wait until she is old enough to decide for herself," said Molly. Adam knew in his limited knowledge that a Christening was also a great excuse for family and friends to get together after a baby was born.

"Today as I walked to the café, so many people stopped me wanting to meet the baby. Now that the weather is nicer, how about we have a house warming cum baby naming party. We could get Harry's pit BBQ over and have a hog roast and beach BBQ, maybe even a clam bake too."

"That's a great idea," said Anna. "What do you think, Molly?"

"Sounds good to me. I love a good party."

"That's all agreed then, I'll chat with Maggie. I'm sure she will be glad to help me organize it and get the necessary permissions."

Invites had been sent and preparations made. Family, friends and many of the local community involved in the café were invited, along with some of Molly's closest friends. Anna and Adam were up early to get the hog roast lit as this would take several hours to cook slowly. The clam-bake pit was dug and filled with stones from the beach.

This was then filled with logs which were lit to heat the stones and let the logs burn away, before it would be layered with seaweed, foiled baked potatoes, and large sheet pans of shellfish, including crabs, lobsters, clams and mussels. This would then be loosely covered in foil and wet sheets before the sand would be placed on top and it would be left to work its magic.

The hay bales were delivered and placed around the beach in front of the house in a large circle. A fire pit had been dug and set up central to this, ready to be lit as the afternoon turned cool. Adam had also set up a large BBQ beside the hog roast for cooking all the usual BBQ fare.

Anna had looked after all the sides, condiments and drinks which were set out on trestle tables to the front of the beach house, and old fashioned oval galvanized steel tubs were dotted around filled with ice and bottles of beer and drinks; each had a bottle opener tied to it.

Anna had also purchased some large beach mats which she had pinned down and added umbrellas and cushion, so Tiffany and any other younger guests would have a place to sit and play.

At 2pm, guests started to arrive and by late afternoon. The celebrations were in full swing, enjoying the location, friends and food. Some guests had brought instruments and were playing as others sang along. Adam lit the fire-pit before he and Anna finally sat down on a bail together and clinked bottles as they looked upon the group of friends and family enjoying themselves.

Molly was sat on the mats with Tiff who had lots of helpers keeping her amused, along with a couple of friends. Anna had also noticed earlier that Molly had caught the eye of one of the young fishermen, who was now sat beside her laughing at something she had said. "Do you remember the hog-roast beach party I had for the opening of the café," asked Anna.

Adam leant in and kissed Anna. "Yes, I do. I remember catching your eye from across the fire for the first time that evening," he smiled and planted her with another kiss.

"That was the start of it all. Just look at the now!" Anna said. Adam put his arm around Anna's shoulder and gently squeezed her to him.

"And what a wonderful now it is," he said.